The Peerless Four

The Peerless Four

Victoria Patterson

COUNTERPOINT | BERKELEY

The timeline is provided by AUWW courtesy of Donna Seymour

Library of Congress Cataloging-in-Publication Data

Patterson, Victoria.
  The Peerless Four : a novel / Victoria Patterson.
    pages cm
  ISBN 978-1-61902-177-8
1. Women athletes–Canada–Fiction. 2. Olympic games–Fiction. 3. Swimming–Competitions–Fiction. 4. Swimming for women–Canada–History–Fiction. 5. Swimming–Canada–History–Fiction. 6. Sport stories. I. Title.

  PS3616.A886P44 2013.
  813'.6–dc23
2013014416

ISBN 978-1-61902-177-8

Cover design by Ann Weinstock
Interior design by Neuwirth & Associates

COUNTERPOINT
1919 Fifth Street
Berkeley, CA 94710
www.counterpointpress.com

Printed in the United States of America
Distributed by Publishers Group West

10 9 8 7 6 5 4 3 2 1

"It's not whether you win or lose but how you play the game."

—Engraved on memorial for Babe Didrikson and
attributed to her

"I don't see any point in playing the game if you don't win."

—Babe Didrikson

"It doesn't really matter if they've forgotten me.
I haven't forgotten them."

—Gertrude Ederle, asked why the world had so quickly
forgotten her as the world's greatest athlete

Let seed be grass, and grass turn into hay:
I'm martyr to a motion not my own;
What's freedom for? To know eternity.
I swear she cast a shadow white as stone.
But who would count eternity in days?
These old bones live to learn her wanton ways:
(I measure time by how a body sways.)

—Theodore Roethke, "I Knew a Woman"

The Peerless Four

The Peerless Four and Hugh Williams
Before the 1928 Olympics

Florence Smith

Basketball brought me to life, and once I was awake and alive, there was no turning back. I'm not good at school, never have been. There's a clarity and straightforwardness to basketball, to sports, that I understand. There are rules. You follow the rules and try to win. Life isn't like that. Too bad, because in life you have to work to make anything make sense. Life is deceptive. In basketball, I'm asked to be smart: to get the ball, pass the ball, fake a pass, dribble, and to shoot the ball through the hoop. When I run, I'm asked to run as fast as I can, beat the others. Cross the finish line first. I have a job to do, and I either get it done or don't. There's nothing vague about it. It's very clear. Life is tough and disappointing and I can't control anything, so to me the best answer is sports. There's no right or wrong answer like with arithmetic. I'm not asked to come up with something like you have to in English. I don't have to decipher a story or a poem. I'm connected to others, and we're connected through time, when it was clear and straightforward then, like it is now. There's no trick answer, nothing that you have to interpret or guess. I don't understand Shakespeare or algebra or why a poem makes people cry, but give me the ball, and I'll dribble and pass, and I'll take the elbow to the face, the lumps and the bruises, gladly, to know that I'm doing something truly fine, something that's as good as Shakespeare, if you ask me, as good as any poem, even better, if you ask me. It's action. It has the kind of power and force of the known, and I gave myself over as soon as I discovered basketball. I knew that I'd found an answer to my life. I was alive.

At first, my dad wouldn't let me play basketball. I was ten and we would go to my brother's games at the high school. I'm the only girl of five children, and being from a family of boys, I did everything that they did, which confused my dad, since it wasn't ladylike. That's how I got into running, because of my three older brothers. I ran to keep away from them.

"I want to do that," I told my dad at the basketball game, and he shook his head and said, "That's not for girls." It's very simple, really. Boys play sports and girls watch the boys play sports. My dad believes that girls should stay home and work and bring the money home until they get married. Girls shouldn't go to college—fine by me! Only the boys should. But I wanted to be on the basketball court, and I didn't care what my dad said.

I'd watch my brother with his squeaking shoes crossing the court, dribbling and passing, making his shots, and he gave meaning to my life, gave me a purpose. I cheered for him with such yearning and enthusiasm that my dad would put his hands on my shoulders, beg me to sit back down. But he couldn't keep me sitting. It was bigger than him, bigger than me. I became so involved in the games, in my desire to break free from life's confusions, to have a purpose within me. It was like I became my brother, and I was in the competitive world of men, and I was important.

Before the games, I couldn't eat because of nerves. I'd pace the house, going over game plans in my head. "Sit down!" my dad would say. "You're making everyone nervous." During the games, I'd pace the stands, clenching my fists, waving my fists, shouting. I couldn't stay still. Cheering is what you call it, but it was more than that. I strutted up and down the aisles, dribbling my imaginary ball with my brother. I faked defenders, turned and made my shots. I took low, sweeping passes. I trotted and swerved and blocked players, careful not to foul. All this I did with a very loud commentary, letting my dad and the spectators and the refs know that I knew everything, that I was in the game, and that I was part of this world whether my dad let me play for real or not. Truly, I believed that my brother depended on me, that in some magical way, I was him, and that his success and his team's depended on my vigilance. When he made a shot, when he passed the ball with beauty, and the crowd clapped and roared, I believed that they were roaring for me, as much as for him. It felt like an assurance that life could be understandable.

I couldn't stop moving and talking and my dad became concerned. People stared, moved away from us. A few stayed, fascinated by my antics.

"You're like a crazy person," my dad said.

Then my dad decided that I couldn't come to the basketball games anymore. My cheering was too much. The games were my delight, my reason for living, and I locked myself in a closet and cried for two days. I refused to eat. My family couldn't get me to come out. Even my brother, whom I love with all my heart, because he believes in me and plays sports with me, and he taught me what he knows about basketball—he couldn't get me to come out. My mom made blueberry pie, my favorite, put it right outside the closet so that I smelled it. But I didn't care.

"Let her play," I heard my mom tell my dad. "Girls play basketball all the time now," said my brother, and my dad said, "Not my daughter." But he gave in, because I wouldn't come out of the closet or eat, and I'm his daughter, and he loves me.

He never watches me compete, but he might take pride. I don't know. Whenever I bring home a ribbon, he says, "Don't get a swelled head," and that's it.

So when it came to letting me go to the Olympics, it was difficult. I wasn't going to be able to have children, he said. Everyone knows that's not true, I said. My grandmother wants to put a chastity belt on me, and she practically disowned my dad when he relented. They're Lutherans and serious. Sturdy, good workers, farmers, and grim about life.

Bonnie Brody

The first time I kissed my coach, he pulled away. The second time I kissed him, he didn't. He tries to blame our relationship on his difficult home life, and on my mother's death, my grief, but the truth is, when we're together, we're not usually thinking about any of these things, and he knows it. We'd known each other for over ten years by then, and he'd watched me grow up. He'd watched me become an athlete and recognized in me the potential for greatness. He said I had rawness, power, grace, and perseverance, and that he wanted to work with me.

The first kiss came after one of our practice sessions. We were in the boys' locker room, no one there but us, and he was leaned up against the wall, his head tilted, smiling a little, even though he was sad, and I didn't think about how he is so much older than me, or that he has a wife and kids, or that I'm only sixteen. I never really worry about these things, even though I know that's what everyone else thinks about, and I'm supposed to as well. He was telling me about his mother. We have the same shape of eyes, and my laugh sounds like hers. His mother died a few years back. He wasn't crying but he looked like he wanted to. The desire I felt for him up to that point had been a childhood crush—harmless and sweet—but it switched, just like that, into something inside my body. Something large and disobedient and not so sweet but more important. It just seemed like an extension of what we had been doing before, with his touching and guiding me, watching me. When I ran, his eyes were on me, and that was what I loved.

Besides, he looked like he needed me to kiss him. He really did. So I leaned in and did so, and when he pulled away, he looked shocked and scared, and he took a step back.

Our next practices we pretended like nothing happened. But I would catch him looking at me strangely, a desiring and haunted look—looking, looking, and looking, and he couldn't stop watching and looking.

Then finally by the lockers, the same spot, I kissed him again, and this time he kissed back. Hard. Pressed against me.

Now we're together.

My running has improved. He only has to gaze at me and I can read his mind, as if he's running through me, instructing me from the inside. I do exactly what he wants, and all the problems with my form, I can correct, because I know what he wants just from his feeling inside me. Elbows closer, head straighter, knees higher, spring faster. I feel so powerful in my body because it belongs to him.

Last week, at the track, he told me that we had to stop. The sun had gone down, no one was out there but us. He could no longer coach me, he said, because he couldn't resist me.

I stared at him, and then I started bouncing on my toes.

"What are you doing?" he asked.

I kept bouncing.

"I love you," he said. "You know that. But this will ruin your life, and mine."

I started to run and he reached for my arm, knowing what I would do, but I shook him loose. He didn't even try to catch me. I'm that fast. He called, "Come back!" but I kept running.

He stood and watched and waited, and every time I'd pass him on my loop, he'd shake his head and look down. Once, I reached out and scratched his neck as I passed. He crossed his hands across his chest, looked at me disapprovingly, but I kept at it, not a jog, but a full-out run.

An hour or more passed, I'm not sure how long. My face and hair were dripping with sweat, but I continued my pace. I wouldn't slow. My leg muscles were trembling and everything was going in and out of focus, but I kept at it.

"Stop!" I heard him yell. "Stop, stop! You're going to hurt yourself!" But I whipped past him. "You'll pull a muscle," he called out, and then finally, "Okay, okay. I take everything back that I said earlier."

When I didn't stop, he yelled, "I take it back!"

I came into my body, realized that he was right—I felt like I was going to die. I lunged to a stop but my legs wouldn't quit, and so I buckled over, going down in the dirt, grasping my knees, coughing, heaving. The sound coming from me was raw and awful, from deep inside, and I was shaking all over.

Coach ran to me, put his hands on my back and neck, legs, arms, all over me, trying to help.

I gasped for breath, watching his solemn face above me, a welt on his neck where my fingers had dug into his skin.

After some time had passed he said, "Okay? Okay, now?"

I nodded because I still didn't have enough breath to speak.

Hugh Williams

Once, after having inhaled a large quantity of nitrous oxide to assist in what was described as a painless procedure, the extraction of two of my rotted molars, I sat in the dentist's chair believing that a piece of the blue sky would climb through the opened window directly in front of me, and into the dentist's room, like a person. Once inside, the sky would walk up to my face and cover my gaping mouth, suffocating me, without anyone able to see it besides me, for it was sky. I was six. My mother waited for me in another room. I had cried for her but they wouldn't let her inside. The sky had the color of light blue and no face but arms and legs and it would stroll up to me and move inside my brain, covering my mouth along the way, until I could no longer breathe. Mid-extraction, I squirmed and resisted, gasping and coughing, the sky moving toward me. I tried to alert the dentist and made a gargled cry for help. Then I cried for my mother but she couldn't hear me. The dentist had large, hairy knuckles, and he called over two assistants. "We've got a live fish," he said. One held my shoulders, the other my legs. A third was summoned to keep my head steady, and before the first extraction was done, hairy knuckles at my face, I lost consciousness, everything dissolving into blackness.

But before that happened, the sky jumped toward me—a flash of brightness—and it was laughing, and then it vaporized like smoke.

This is what it feels like to run. No matter how good of shape I'm in, during a race, the lights go on and off. In my mind. I see blurry things all the way. I never ran when that didn't happen.

Maybe the sky did enter me that day in the dentist's chair, because when I awoke, I was different. I was in bed and when I turned my head, the first thing I saw was my mother, and I knew then that I would do anything to keep her near me. My tongue probed for the usual soreness of the molars and was met with a soft hollow of gums. The accompanying throbbing inside my head was now cottony and numbed. There was a great relief, as if ten pounds of weight had been removed from my face. This sensation, too, is like running for me, when I'm done, having crossed the tape to completion, and to the exaltation of my mother and Coach.

I started running because my mother told me that I either had to learn how to fight or to run. "It's as simple as that," she said, because I'm scrawny. So I learned to run. I thought it was the easier thing to do. I was always very perceptive and sensitive, and I used to cry in the high school bathroom. Then I started running so I wouldn't have to fight. Of course I didn't know anything about technique. I'd never even seen a track meet. Then one day Coach saw me and timed me. He took his watch to the repair place because he thought it was broken, but it wasn't.

Coach told me that I'm a child of nature, and that my ability comes directly from Christ our Father. Like I said, I'm skinny and small and no one would ever mistake me for an athlete, so maybe he's right. But I got those rotted teeth from God as well.

Coach believes I run best on hate, and once before a race, when I was just beginning to compete and hadn't won yet, he forged a letter from my father, who'd left my mother and me sometime after I was born. A no-good musician, and I never met him that I remember.

In the letter, my dad said that he had never loved me or my mother and that I couldn't possibly win the race, and then Coach signed it Your Father. I knew that it was from Coach because he crossed his t's downward like Coach and he probably knew that I knew. But I got angry like it was from my father, and I probably did that for Coach, because I would do anything for him. Building up my ego has a lot to do with winning, and the only thing that drives my legs is my mind and my desire. So I think about Coach and Mother. He and Mother are the happiest when I win.

The next morning after stewing all night in hate over that letter that I knew in my head was forged but kept in my heart as real, I licked the track with my feet in the 100-metres, beating the second runner by five yards.

But that one time, when I crossed the tape, I came down and there was no relief, no numbed and cottony feeling, no weight lifted, and Coach was at my side.

I love that man like a father.

Coach, I said. What's wrong with me?

Breathe, he said. Stretch out.

I can't, I said. It hurts.

What hurts? he asked. Is it a cramp?

No, I said. I can't breathe. Then I whispered: Please let this be over. I don't like this.

What? he asked. What, what?

I can't breathe, I said. Please, let this be over.

No, Hugh, he said. You're just beginning.

I started to cry.

Stop, he said. You're a champion. Stop crying.

The sky, I said.

What?

The sky. It's inside me, and I can't breathe.

The sky? he said.

Yes. The sky.

That's enough, he said. You're a winner. You're a champion.

I don't care, I said.

I care, he said. Your mother cares.

He shook his head in confusion, raised my arms above my head. He begged me to stop talking nonsense, said it scared him. No more crying, he said. He bent my knees toward my chest, stretched out my legs.

Just let go, he said. Unclench. You're all clenched up.

I did what he said, and I never burdened him with crazy-talk about the sky again.

Ginger Hadley

One day, when I was six years old, my father reluctantly gave me permission to try the high jump in our backyard. I always liked to jump things. We have a fence around our yard, and when I got older, I never went through the gate. I always jumped it. My older brothers used the high jump, and I wanted to try even though I was too young. My dad set the bar as low as it would go. I waited until I was alone. I didn't want anyone watching me. When I reached the jump, I was afraid. I hesitated, and then I barreled into the bar. Before I could block it with my hands, the bar hit the back of my head. The accident left a scar several inches long. Today I barely notice it. Sometimes I forget what side it's on.

After my dad stitched the cut, he gave me a rag doll. I still have it. Soon the high jump became my greatest preoccupation, more than anything else. It's amazing how many times I can try and not make it; then, after I make it once, it becomes easy, and I have to try for more.

Later, when I beat my record and everyone else's, my dad gave me his ukulele. I don't know how to play but I'm teaching myself.

Quiet, shy, forlorn, pretty. These are the things people say about me. For the most part, they're true.

Muriel Ziegler

I was eleven when I saw from the stands a man down near the green and brown of the lacrosse field, drunk and staggering. My parents had taken me to the game for my birthday because that was what I wanted. No dolls or dresses or anything like that, ever. I watched him for a long time as he eyed the players and watched the game. He swayed, mumbling to himself, hands in his big trench-coat pockets. A former player? Coach gone crazy? A fan? I went through the possibilities but none seemed to fit. How did he get so close to the field? I watched and wondered for a long time. Then, to my shock, he made a great running break for the game. I sat up straight, a tingling sensation through my spine. A line of men at the field blocked the drunken man. He was thrust back, and the men watched him. He seemed to accept his defeat, glowering, turning, and walking away. They all went back to watching the game, but not me. I watched the man. He paused. His shoulders went down, as if sensing something. Then he turned and made another great leaping run, his coat flapping behind him. He lunged but he couldn't break through. Three of them had him, and he struggled in their clutches. He broke free, made another lunge—but they thrust him back and then tackled him. By this time, I wasn't the only one watching, the crowd jeering and cheering and laughing. My mom said, "What a shame," and she put her warm hand at the back of my neck. "Poor sot," my dad mumbled. "He's gonna get killed." But the man wasn't done. Somehow, he tricked them into letting go of him a little, maybe making them think he was calmed. He managed to shake free, and he was up again, bursting through, running head-on into the field. Inside I shouted Go! Go! Go! even as I understood he'd disrupted the game, players moving to the sides. But he had a purpose that we didn't understand; I tried but I could only sense it. Quarter-field, the man slowed and a policeman ran from behind him, caught his arm, and slung him down in a tackle. The crowd cheered. A pack of security men hurried to assist, and they lifted him, hauling him—twisting and kicking the whole way—off the field. At one point, he almost got loose again—Go! Go! Go!—but there were just too many of them.

The game was back on but I continued to watch the man. I had to turn my body all the way around and watch behind me, away from the field and at the parking lot. All the other heads in the stands were turned to the game except mine. The policeman restrained the man with handcuffs behind his back, and then the officer and the security men took him—carried him, truth be told, his feet off the ground—to a police car. I saw that there was a bloody gash at his cheek. A security man placed his hand on the man's head and pushed hard, and the policeman used a baton to make his knees buckle, so that he squat-sat into a forced position in the backseat. After the door shut, the side of his head pressed against the glass of the window, a splotch of hair and skin. Then the car started, drove off, and he was gone.

The man never gave up. He never gave up.

When I was a little girl, my mom read to me at night about Jack going up the beanstalk and killing that giant, and Little Red Riding Hood getting the better of that Big Bad Wolf, and runty David slaying nine-foot Goliath with nothing but a rock and courage, and many other stories that as I got older, I realized weren't true, weren't facts. People invented the stories to console us. The weaker don't win. The giants do. But I decided, like the drunken man, that even if I couldn't beat down Fate, that I would rock it back on its heels as much as I could, putting my entire body and heart into the blows. I would get joy from it. I would taste what it means to be free.

I had my first real test three days after I witnessed the drunken man. For just about three minutes in the afternoon after school. It was at the back of an empty parking lot when I fought Jimmy Harper, the school bully, and almost won, with a crowd of kids watching. No sooner had I challenged Harper to the fight than I was certain that he'd win, as surely as I knew that the stars would be out that night and the sun up the next morning. He was bigger than me, older. He was a boy. He knew how to fight. But I challenged him anyway. He wasn't bullying me but I was sick and tired of him bullying others.

There is nothing to compare to that flash of power I felt when my right hand smacked into his jaw. His head went back and his eyes flamed and I knew right then that victory should not be confused with winning. Something even better came from losing, from almost winning. That some might mistake it as a tragedy but not me: weak, pitiful, helpless, insignificant no more.

Harper was a big, ugly, angry kid, two years older than me, and he sprung and tightened like a coil, came back at me, hitting with a whistling left-handed hook. I ducked but it caught the side of my head and I went dizzy. He was a blurring of arms and fists, battering at me, and I knew it was over. But then I heard the kids yelling my name, wanting me to take him, and I realized there weren't any of them cheering for Harper. Not anymore. It would be like rooting for the seeing man in a shootout against a blind man, the second before the blind man gets shot in the heart. I was smiling and smiling when I went down to the ground, nose broken, face bloodied, and the fight ended. About three minutes had passed. Harper won but he wasn't smiling like me. He seemed a little shocked by it all.

After that, I went after everything full force, whether I won or not. It didn't matter and the only thing that mattered was the feeling I got from it.

I joined the Athletic Club, and when I first ran at the Canadian National Exhibition in Toronto, I didn't have my running clothes or shoes with me, and there were no stores that carried track and field attire for women. So I wore my brother's swimming trunks, my father's socks, and a gym jersey, and I borrowed a pair of shoes from one of the boys. I placed first in the discus, the javelin, the shot put, the 220, and the 120-yard low hurdles, and second in the 100-yard dash, despite never having been coached in the discus, shot put, or javelin.

I watched the boys who went before me, and then tried to do what they did. I don't know how I did it, to be honest. I just had the feeling like I could do anything. Really, we girls didn't know what we were doing. We had to try to work things out for ourselves. We were the first ones to try, so there was no one to copy. And it was then that I was told that I would go to the Olympics.

But none of this would have been possible had I not decided that I didn't need victories and championships. I just wanted to rock Fate back on its heels and taste freedom.

I'll always remember how Harper won that fight but I got all the glory. They were calling my name, not his, and I had the feeling like the drunken man whom they couldn't stop at the lacrosse field, fierce and not ever giving up. Call it tragic, call it losing, but I say it's all victory.

Toronto Daily Star
Editorials, June 1928

We feel that the Olympic Games must be reserved for the solemn and periodic manifestation of male athleticism with internationalism as a base, loyalty as a means, arts for its setting, and female applause as reward.

—Baron Pierre de Coubertin, esteemed founder of the modern
Olympic Games, and the International Olympic Committee

No female should be seen swaggering around, pretending to be male. If females must compete in the Olympics, they should be consigned to participating in ladylike sports that allow them to look beautiful and wear some pretty cute costumes: archery, figure skating, and horseback riding being the best examples—activities that would not cause them to perspire. Furthermore, there is scientific evidence that the rigors of athletic activities weaken women for motherhood.

I happened to encounter the so-called Peerless Four while sitting at the counter of a Toronto restaurant that shall remain unnamed. I was having a cup of chicken soup and a grilled cheese sandwich when it occurred to me from my quick glance that the party of seven seated in a booth a few stools away from me included the Peerless Four, along with their sponsor, a large man I later found out is a dubious character by the name of Jack Grapes, and a female chaperone whom I know from social circles, Mrs. Ross, married to Dr. W. R. Ross, and one more, a female of unknown connection, though my conjecture is that she is a sibling to one of the four.

My eyes on my soup, I listened to their animated chatter about their upcoming trip to Amsterdam. When I finally did look up, I almost jumped from my stool at the sight of Muriel Ziegler.

Ziegler is the leader of a breed of women that is more man than woman, and more sexually uncertain than heterosexual. I saw a thin-skinned, masculine face with a slit for a mouth, hawkish nose, and black eyes. She happens to have a man's body, and one is not sure whether to use the address of Miss, Mrs., Mr., or It. She acts like a man, sounds like a man, *looks* like a man.

One gets the impression that Ziegler chooses to compete against women in athletic contests simply because she would not or could not compete at their best and most noble game—courting and marrying a man. Athletics are an escape, compensation, because without athletic contests, she'd have no way to catch a man's eye.

Next to Ziegler was Ginger Hadley—the Dream Girl—unmistakably. Now I understand why she is called that name. She was dressed in a blue dress, more like a gown, long and drape-like, very graceful and floaty, with a charming sweater and hat, and I saw no evidence of the masculinity that burdened her peers. Her black silky hair curled out from her hat, she has porcelain skin and a bow-shaped mouth, and her figure is long, lean, and perfectly shaped. I was only able to give her four or five frantic glances. She has the type of dazzling beauty that you can't linger on too long. It makes the observer feel indecent.

I had an overwhelming desire to free her. How this would be accomplished, I had no idea. I wanted to say, "With your beauty you demonstrate that in athletics women don't belong. It would be much better for you to stay home, get yourself prettied up, and let that phone ring. For undoubtedly it will! You are a stunner, a glamour girl!" I didn't, of course, say anything.

The one named Bonnie Brody wouldn't have been called good-looking, certainly not by this judge. She seems to be built satisfactorily, but she wore an awful bulky skirt and blouse, socks to her calves, as if to make one forget her immediately. She made awkward, almost violent gestures when she spoke, and she had an absolute buzzing intensity that loaded her young features with an aged severity. Her short hair ringed out from her head in a wild and electric manner, as if fleeing her brain.

The fourth, Florence Smith, has the demeanor and shape of a ten-year-old boy. Yet she has the high-pitched giggle of a ten-year-old girl. She strikes me as foolish and easily swayed. She wore a flower clipped in her hair as if to offset the masculine. If she is not careful, she is bound to become a she-man like Ziegler.

Mrs. Ross, their chaperone, once prepared a delicious meal for a party of six that included me as one of Dr. Ross's dinner guests, a business-related invitation, the details of which are unrelated.

I remembered Mrs. Ross's sober intent dark-eyed stare from that dinner, and at first I wasn't sure that the woman at the restaurant was the same Mrs. Ross, for that afternoon she wore a hat low to her brow, so that it was a challenge to see her face.

But then, from her place at the table, she turned her attention to me, and there was no mistaking her stare. Her commanding dark eyes took me in, with a seeming indifference.

I shook my head in question to her, as if to say, Why? and she gave no acknowledgement, and then she turned away.

I remembered how she wore a blue apron that night, and how after the dinner plates had been cleared, and as we waited for coffee and dessert, through an open doorway to the kitchen, we saw that she sat with a book beside a lamp at the kitchen table. So consumed was she by what she read, she did not hear her husband calling for her, and we at the dining room table had a nice chuckle about the situation.

Finally, Dr. Ross had to stand and go to her, and when she came back to the dining room table bearing a platter of cobbler, she apologized in earnest for neglecting her duties as our hostess.

Mrs. Ross is a distracted but otherwise dutiful wife. Her presence at that restaurant table, in all honesty, confounds me. Yet it is also a small comfort to know that the girls will have a significant female example. She and Dr. Ross have no children of their own. Her maternal instincts have found the opportunity to bloom, however misguided the destination.

I found my disgust steered toward the sponsor, Jack Grapes, a man around my age though more than twice my size, and I wanted to shout at him, "Listen, you son of a gun, what do you think you're doing? How dare you corrupt these youths!" I was so upset, I could no longer continue to eat, and left to pay for my meal with the cashier.

Soon enough, Mr. Grapes was standing right next to me, waiting to pay the cashier as well. Unable to resist, I turned my head to face him. When he looked at me, I said, "So you're going to Amsterdam, are you?" and my face and voice were full of scorn, because he answered back, "What's your problem, buddy?" He looked at me mockingly, then he smiled a terrible, ingratiating smile, and I walked out the door shaking with anger, overwhelmed by my fears for these girls.

The Peerless Four are a disgrace to athletes. They need our protection, not our support. Ziegler is too far-gone, but the others might be saved from a fate such as hers.

The ancient Greeks kept women out of their Games entirely, even as spectators. If caught, a woman was to be thrown off a mountain.

I'm not suggesting that we go back to this approach, but I am suggesting that perhaps the ancient Greeks were right to protect their male athletes. With de Coubertin's resignation, the Games are under threat. When we allow females a few acceptable competitions, they only end up demanding more.

Sincerely,

Edward P. Brundage

Chapter One
Backyard Jumper

I was in Jack Grapes's Cadillac, with Jack driving. A sleek black Cadillac that reminded me of a hearse, the motor thrumming beneath us. Ginger Hadley and her sister Danielle, or Danny, as everyone called her, in the backseat. Hazy beams of sunlight flickered through the trees. Behind us on the road, another car followed with a photographer and Sam Sacks, the high-jump coach whom Jack had hired to train Ginger for the 1928 Olympics, even though Ginger swore that she didn't need him. Seventeen years old and she knew everything. She did what came natural, she said, scissoring those legs so that she flew-stepped across the bar. Jack was sponsoring Ginger, and Danny was part of the package.

I watched Jack using his thumbs to steer on the straight shot of the road, his big thigh next to me flexing now and then. He was unusually quiet. The photographer would snap the Dream Girl (they'd already started calling Ginger that), in her shack of a house in Beechy, Saskatchewan, drumming up more support and money, and Jack would soothe the sisters' father. Jack had it all figured out, and he was silent now, mulling it over.

His hand left the steering wheel and went inside his jacket, fingering a flask nestled in the lining of his inside pocket. His eyes glimmered in my direction and he sucked in his cheeks, blew some air through his mouth.

When I moved to Canada from Ohio, my suitcase handle was engraved with my initials M.E.L. (Marybelle Eloise Lee). The train steward looked at my suitcase and called me Mel, and I took the name because it fit me more than the other. I glimmered my eyes back, letting Jack know that I had my own flask, fitted tightly in the garter at my thigh, its metal cool against my skin.

"You're something else, Mel," he said, staring straight ahead.

Jack was the founder of the Parksdale Ladies Athletic Club. Jack is Irish and Scottish with some French and Italian thrown in. A former professional hockey player and a self-made mining millionaire, with brokerage firms where he didn't work much and where he employed amateur women athletes whether they had skills or not. Typists, stenographers, and mailers, women in their late teens and early twenties worked for Jack and played for his basketball team, advertising his business.

Jack had a knack for getting people to hand over their money. Forty-two with a patch of scalp near the back of his silvery-haired head that had decided, after all, not to go bald, he wore a brown fedora, insecure about that one naked spot. The bridge of his nose flattened and switched directions midway, lending an appealing confusion to his features, and a scar pitted his freshly shaved jawline. His big dark sleepy eyes had an inward look that opened itself to me in dazzling flashes.

I threw a glance and a smile back at the sisters, sitting close, thighs touching and bodies vibrating with the engine. Danny was holding Ginger's hand in her lap. I could never remember which sister was older. They were giving themselves over to their thoughts, as if they were one person. Maybe thinking about all that had happened since they were girls, Ginger jumping the caragana hedges between their home and the end of the street, Danny racing beside her. Or thinking about how Ginger was the runt of the family, until Mother Nature bestowed her in her sixteenth year with eight inches of height, so that her father raised the jumping bar he'd assembled in their backyard. That year, Ginger told me, she'd lie in bed and *feel* herself grow.

They had matching wavy bobbed black hair but Danny was a plainer version of Ginger, broader and wider-hipped, less sharp-featured. All the things that stood out with Ginger—her eyes, hair, body, lips—seemed unrealized, as if the same features had stagnated. Yet there was a lonely mysterious vacancy to Ginger. Her aloofness attracted men and came across as poise, but I couldn't help but feel that there was something sinister behind it.

Danny, on the other hand, was ever-present and practical, and that afternoon, she leaned forward, asking, "Can we stop at Beechy Drugstore for a Coke?"

"Sure thing," Jack said.

"It's coming up," she said, leaning back, satisfied. Sure it was coming up. There wasn't much along Main Street: a post office, a grocery, a café, a bank, and oceans of fields with the South Saskatchewan River a distant shimmering ribbon.

We parked in the dirt parking lot, and the car that was following slowed and parked near us. Jack motioned for Sacks and the photographer to stay in the car. The sky was big and blue and bright, and a couple of fat cows behind a fence raised their heads, watching us with mild interest, mouths chewing in a sideways motion.

When Ginger got out of the Cadillac, she stood for a second, smoothing her skirt on her hips. Birds squawked and twittered and there was a rustling noise in a bush. She presented her mouth discreetly for Danny, and Danny gave a head nod, indicating that there were no lipstick flecks on her teeth.

We entered the drugstore, Jack holding the door open. A bell rang above the door but the people inside were already watching, as if waiting, a few of the mothers at the ice cream counter holding napkins to their kids' mouths.

Jack took his hat in his hand, his hair a little damp against his forehead. We stood there, and then the girl ladling ice cream looked up. She set the scoop back in its water and came around the counter. "Hold on," she said, and she hurried to a back room.

She came back with a small man in a white coat. His glance slid right off me. The gazes of men had been directed at me for years, but at thirty-eight, I knew that this stage of my life was ending.

The druggist's fist disappeared in Jack's pumping handshake and introductions were made. When it was over, the druggist turned to the people at the counter and said, "Folks, it's the Dream Girl!" but they didn't need the pharmacist to tell them who Ginger was. A young girl, probably about ten, was about as happy-looking as I'd ever seen a person.

The pharmacist said to Ginger, "Your photographs don't do you justice."

It wasn't a cold look that Ginger gave him but there wasn't warmth. She turned her gaze from him, and her fingers passed over her throat.

"Hello, girls," came a voice, and soon an older woman at the far end of the drugstore came forward, tall and gaunt with a wolfish face. She reached a limp hand out, and first Danny shook it by the fingers, then Ginger. "How've you been?" she asked, and the sisters nodded, indicating that they'd been good.

Wolf-woman looked around at us and she said, "I had the pleasure of teaching the Hadley girls from first grade to sixth." The sisters were looking down, as if in somber remembrance.

"Good girls," Wolf-woman continued. "Not bookish. Polite. Never spoke out of turn. Ladylike." She gave a burdensome sigh, and then she shook her head.

"What is it?" Jack asked, smiling with curiosity.

Even before she spoke, I knew what was coming. "I'm afraid," she said, conferring a benevolent stare upon the sisters, "that I worry." She went on like this, telling us that she agreed with Baron Pierre de Coubertin. Female participation in the Games, she said, was another example of the disturbing changes occurring in postwar Canada. Women possessed the vote, they smoked, used makeup—and here she looked pointedly at Ginger—went everywhere without chaperones. Where would it end?

Wanting to protect the sisters and not knowing what else to do, I moved forward, so that the sisters would feel my presence.

Wolf-woman assessed me, and then she showed her displeasure with a chortling noise. She tried to shame me by letting her eyes linger over my wedding band, to Jack's wedding-ring-less hand, and then back upon my face. But I was beyond shame, and I sensed the sisters behind me.

Then I heard Ginger say in a quiet voice, "I just want to win."

"You have a good day, now," Jack said.

Wolf-woman thanked him with a forced patience while throwing a shifty look at me. She said good-bye to the sisters and retreated. The pharmacist gave us Cokes with straws, insisting that they were "on the house," though Jack tipped him enough to pay for four more.

Before we left, the happy girl had Ginger sign her handkerchief with a leaky fountain pen, and Ginger pressed her lips to the cloth, leaving a flowery-red kiss print beneath her name.

Back in the Cadillac, Jack revved the engine and there was a gravelly noise beneath our tires as we pulled out from the parking lot, the other car following. I was sad, and for some reason thinking about Kallipateira sneaking into those ancient Games, anxious to watch her son, a boxer, compete. After all, she'd trained him after his father had died. I thought about telling the story to Jack and the sisters but inside the car was a quiet contentment that I didn't want to sabotage. Kallipateira had dressed as a male trainer and stood in the crowd. When her son won, she was so excited, she jumped over a barrier to congratulate him, snagging her robe and exposing her womanhood, ensuring a future rule: trainers had to enter the Games naked to prove that they were indeed men. Fortunately, because Kallipateira's father, three brothers, nephew, and son were Olympic victors, the officials decided not to kill her.

We'd gone about a half-mile in silence when Jack tapped his palm against the horn, muttering, "Move it, move it," and a furry beast scattered across the road. Jack swerved and missed it. He slowed, and up ahead I saw a brick schoolhouse amid the trees, where Wolf-woman had no doubt taught the sisters to be quiet and ladylike. Seeing the schoolhouse made me remember all the way back to when I was nine, and I'd first moved to Toronto with my suitcase with M.E.L. on the handle, to live with my father after my mother had passed from cancer and my grandparents didn't want to keep me. My father was a reporter and a drinker, and I wanted him to love me, even though he had left my mom. He kept bottles in his trunk, and a wad of cash in a thick rubber band, and all of this flashed through me, but I was able to leave it at the schoolhouse in the trees when we passed.

Jack made the turn that meant we were close, and he leaned toward me and said, "Friday, golf."

"Name?" I asked, knowing that this meant he'd made an appointment to play golf with Florence Smith's father, for the same reason we were going to the sisters' house now.

"Walter Smith," he said. "A sweet tooth. Flo says he loves coconut."

I had my notebook out now and I wrote down the name, adding, *Macaroons.*

"Snappy dresser," Jack said. "Changes clothes during the day. Flo says he reads the Bible to them every night."

"Okay," I said, writing, *Dandy Jesus Lover.*

I was always writing in my notebooks. I'd gotten a taste for filling one after the other, and then locking them in my closet, because they weren't anything I wanted my husband to read. Wallace swore he wouldn't touch them, let alone read them, if you paid him. He didn't want to know what was inside. Now that I was living with the girls, I kept the books locked in a safety deposit box at the bank. I used to report on women's sports for the *Toronto Daily News,* but that had little to do with what I put in those notebooks. Spilling myself on those blank pages had become a habit.

Jack drove about a mile along an unpaved road with our dust storm behind us for the car following, and then he pulled the Cadillac over. The house was a two-story with a wide front porch, the wood old and paint-chipped, set back from the road, with a wire fence around a yard. I recognized a maple and an old oak. The grass was overgrown and a half-dozen or so hens clucked in a pen. An ancient black dog lay in a heap at the porch. It was one of those houses with chickens and sleeping dogs and something lonely and average about it.

As we walked closer, I saw that the side was being repainted and in the process of repairs. I wondered if this had to do with the money that Jack had given the sisters.

By the time we opened the gate, Mr. Hadley was on the front porch coming toward us. But then he stopped and waited, a very tall man, thin, wearing a suit like Jack's, with a blue shirt underneath. We got closer and I saw that his face had that same remote look that Ginger's has, making me wonder if it was something genetic and not about a hurt, but then the look passed and he was shaking Jack's hand, hugging his girls, and nodding a welcoming hello at me. He had the same deep brown eyes as his girls, and he'd shaved before we arrived, fresh nicks of crusted blood along his jawline.

Jack introduced Sam Sacks, who limped forward and said that he was delighted to meet Mr. Hadley, absolutely delighted, and then Jack turned his attention to me, introducing me by my full name, not as Mel, and explaining that I was married to Dr. W. R. Ross, not only an esteemed doctor, but also the Canadian representative for the International Amateur Athletic Federation. With de Coubertin's influence diminished, five track and field events had been opened for women. On a trial basis—an experiment, and the IAAF would vote afterward. He explained that I was chaperoning the ladies everywhere, living with them, and that Mr. Hadley could rest easy, knowing that I was with his girls at all times.

As we stood talking, occasionally a flash would go off, and Mr. Hadley would squint, as if someone had pinched him. He'd sent his kids and wife to his aunt's house, he explained, so that we'd have quiet. Jack was disappointed, thinking of the missed photo opportunities, but he had his game face on, and no one could tell but me. Ginger crouched to pet the dog, whose name was Lucky, and the flashbulbs started. Lucky made no response. I was beginning to wonder if the dog was dead, but then I saw his rib cage lift with breath. The photographer wanted a better shot of Lucky and Ginger communing, and Danny tried to help, murmuring Lucky's name, encouraging him to sit, bringing out a piece of ham, but nothing worked. Finally, she lifted the dog from his hips and placed him in an awkward sit. Mangy and sick, his yellow tongue hanging from his mouth. Ginger's affection was replaced with a frank disgust at the smell of his breath, so the photographer gave up.

We made our way to the living room, where we sat and talked some more. By the way that Danny and Mr. Hadley were looking at Ginger, I saw that they loved her with a similar awe. All his kids were athletes, Mr. Hadley told us, and he'd had his day, but nothing like Ginger. I imagined them watching her in the backyard jumping that high jump Mr. Hadley had assembled, _for_ hours. Mr. Hadley gave Ginger money when she passed her record, and she kept going. Then one afternoon she jumped five feet three inches, setting a world record. They didn't know it was a world record; it was just her best jump. But Jack found out about her and came and talked up her parents and took her and her sister with him. She'd never jump that high again, not even at the Olympics when she'd win her gold.

The conversation in the living room waned, and I wasn't sure if we'd made headway with Mr. Hadley. Ginger and Danny had been in the kitchen, and then they were upstairs in the bedroom that they'd shared. There was a pause and we heard their feet along the stairway coming down. The sisters practically ran into the room and stood beside their father, who sat stiff-backed, and Ginger kissed his cheek and said, "I love you so much, Poppa," and Danny said, "It's so exciting, Poppa!" kissing his other cheek. Mr. Hadley looked stunned. I smiled at Jack and he was beaming because we both knew that the sisters would go to Amsterdam.

The photographer wanted to snap Ginger in the backyard next to her homemade high jump but she refused. "Why not?" he asked, and Ginger was quiet, but then she whispered something in Danny's ear, and Danny said, "What's the point? It's stupid."

Mr. Hadley said that he had jumping clothes that she could change into, but her face turned red. She agreed to go outside— no photos—and we stood and looked and cast glances at each other while the wind swept the tops of the trees. Mr. Hadley had created a high jump with soft dirt to buffer falls. He'd make Ginger—from age seven on, freckles on her nose, flicking hair from her eyes—come back inside. If she'd had her way, she would have stayed out all night, her breath catching in her chest, and a rushing sound when she flew over the bar, like a wave crashing in her head. A restlessness temporarily released. Hours and hours. Over and over. An ascetic discipline. The reality struck me as vapid and primitive, pursued with a tunnel-like small vision. I wanted it to be noble and profound but there it was, far more strange and pointless.

"She'd rather jump," Mr. Hadley said, "than eat or play or anything."

We went back to the living room, and the photographer fired off more flashes. He moved Ginger and posed her, and she got her lost look that made her pretty, but also made me imagine someone locking her in a closet when she was just a little kid, or touching her where she wasn't supposed to be touched. He stood her beside a bookshelf, pretending to read; sat her at the kitchen table, lifting a teacup; had her pretend to wash the dishes.

I wandered outside to the backyard, the back screen door thumping behind me. The neighbor kids were playing tag or hide-and-seek or something, their excited voices and laughter lifted in the air. I couldn't see them but there were some swoop-backed horses in a field, heads lowered, nibbling at the grass. In the distance was a giant tree, its roots slinking everywhere, and I decided to go to it. Leaves crunched beneath my feet, and I came to an old gate, half-buried, and opened it with a creak. A downward slope led to the tree, and when I got to it, I sat, leaning my back against its trunk, and I looked off into the woods below, the tops of the trees an endless green. A gust of wind set their leaves shaking the same direction, then shifted and rattled them another. To my right was a sea of green-gold wheat and some hills split by the sky. The sun was going down—a fat red ball falling behind the hills. The air smelled like earth and trees and a little bit like manure, probably from those horses. I knew I should go back inside but I didn't want to leave.

I bent my knees and opened my legs so that my dress flopped between my thighs. My brassiere pinched at my side and I adjusted. I reached beneath my dress, unhinged my flask, uncapped it, and took a pull, leaned back. My eyes closed and the whiskey's warmth sank and exploded in a gut-leveling burst.

There were crunching footsteps in the distance, the creak of a gate. I kept my eyes shut, went deep inside myself, a coping technique that I'd developed as a kid. My mom used to say, Where'd you slip away to? So we came to call these my Slip Aways, and the Slip Aways happened even more after she died.

I couldn't express it then, but now I understand that I had an impression that a void was underneath everything. I couldn't make the void disappear or change, but by closing my eyes and concentrating, I managed to balance, like stroking death while escaping life. I closed my eyes and pushed life away. Teachers, principals, students, and most everyone did not approve.

The steps came closer and a body neared but I didn't look. A shifting of weight beside me, and then an arm touching mine.

We sat silent, and I opened my eyes. We watched the sky change colors together, and the person's breathing was labored. When the person leaned forward, I knew that it was Jack retrieving the flask from the inside pocket of his jacket. But I knew it was Jack even before that. A gurgling noise as he took a long swallow, and then a pause before he leaned beside me again, saying, "An athlete is as good as his diet. Whiskey is the worst. Do you drink alcohol, Mrs. Ross?"

I said that I did, and then I lifted my flask to my mouth.

"Weakening your nervous system," he said, looking at the sky. The sunset colors were reaching majestic levels, the breeze cool and sweet. He'd taken his hat off and placed it beside him. "The human body provides its own stimulants, adrenaline and the like. Whiskey clogs your brain, dulls your reflexes, and withers your lungs and heart."

He paused to drink, and then he reached inside his jacket, extracting a silver cigarette case engraved with his initials. He pulled out two hand-rolled cigarettes, saying, "Do you smoke, Mrs. Ross?" He placed both in his mouth and lit them with a single flame, handing me one without waiting for my answer.

"Tobacco," he went on, blowing smoke, "is the body's enemy. Your lungs become a chimney, and there's no chimney sweep to clear the soot."

We were quiet for a long while, smoking and drinking and enjoying the coloring sky. Then he took off his jacket, folded it beside his hat. He pulled his sleeve past his bicep, held out his arm and flexed.

"Feel it," he said. I shook my head, and he said, "Go on."

So I did, putting my hand on his arm and pressing. His muscle was like a piece of wood.

Our cigarettes were hanging from our mouths, his flapping at his lip when he spoke. I let go of his arm and blew my smoke, and then he did the same. He rolled his sleeve down. His eyes had a smile in them, and something sly and guilty. He blinked and just like that, his eyes changed to meditative.

"Strength," he said, "is not in the muscles. It's the mind." He tapped a finger to his skull. "The mind prevails over the body, demands it accomplish the impossible. We must feed the mind. Do you understand, Mrs. Ross?"

He required no response.

"The Olympics," he said, shaking his head sadly. "Politics, money, corruption. It's the secret meaning inside that matters. The inside battle. The sacred meaning inside us . . ." He was losing his concentration.

He took another pull from his flask, a hit from his cigarette. He coughed, looked down. "Winning's easy," he said. "It's secondary. Do you understand? It's the secret meaning inside us. The sacred that matters."

He looked up, attempting a smile that looked more like a wince. "Winning," he said, tapping a long ash, "is not that different from losing, and losing's far more important." He paused in contemplation. "Winning feels good but it doesn't last. Losing feels bad and that feeling lasts."

I took a long drink from my flask while he watched. He continued staring. "After all these years," he said, "I've got something that's larger than myself and connected to me. Something that I know how to do that's not about me. It's bigger than me." His head tilted. "Is that why you're here? I still can't figure out why you're here."

He waited for me to respond but I said nothing.

"C'mon, Mel," he said, looking between his knees. Then he muttered, "It's only a game but it's the only game."

I couldn't look at his face so I focused on the sunset. "I can't go to Amsterdam," I said.

"Why not?"

"Wallace," I said.

"What about him?"

"He wants me home."

Jack didn't speak after that. A sliver of a new moon became visible. We sat and listened to the sounds of the kids' voices and then someone clanged a bell, calling them inside for supper.

Jack sighed and put his hat on, set his flask back in its pocket. He lifted himself with a grunt, held his hand out for me. I took his help, and we went back inside.

Chapter Two
Amazon

———◆———

Two weeks later, I accompanied Jack in his Cadillac, driving to the Royal York Golf Club in Toronto, a plate of macaroons wrapped in a handkerchief on my lap. When Jack took the curves, I held them more securely.

"It's a hell of a thing," Jack said.

"Yes."

"Convincing these men."

"Sure."

"Mothers don't object."

"They speak through the fathers."

"This one should be easy."

"Emphasize the glory."

"I have the impression," he said, "that he wants to play golf, and that's it."

"Easy," I agreed.

"Not like Dr. Ross," he said. We planned to speak with my husband that evening.

I said nothing.

"That's why I pay you," he said, nodding at the cookies.

"You barely pay me," I said, and he laughed.

"I'm beginning to wonder," he said, "what you look like without that hat."

"The same."

"It practically covers your entire face."

"That's true," I said, because that was why I appreciated cloche hats.

We were quiet, the motor whirring and ticking, specks of light freckling us from outside, our clubs rattling in the trunk. Jack wore plaid knickers. I had on a pleated skirt and a sweater vest. He was pensive, about to say something and then hesitating.

"What is it, Jack?"

His head went back and he said, "Nothing, nothing." He was quiet again, and after a few minutes had passed, he said, "I didn't know that you were a runner."

"I was," I said. I couldn't leave it alone, so I asked, "Who told you?"

"That doesn't matter," he said.

We were quiet for a few more minutes, and then he resumed his struggle to speak, so I said, "It's simple. I quit."

"Why?"

"Who told you?"

"I asked around."

"Are you investigating me?"

He gave a sad smile and his eyes stayed on the road.

We turned a corner, and the Royal York clubhouse came into view. A low fog layered the grass, the sun eating it up, and we parked alongside the other cars in the parking lot.

Walter Smith, as it turned out, appreciated my macaroons, but he didn't want me on the golf course with the men. "We aren't closed-door," he said. "Girls are encouraged to come out and have lunch. Really, the only thing they're not encouraged to do is to play the golf course."

Jack turned a face full of apology to me but I nodded for him to go ahead. Instead of waiting at the clubhouse, I sat in Jack's Cadillac with my window opened, listening to the repeating cracks of the clubs hitting the balls.

Summer was here: the days getting longer, hotter, drier, and windier. A hawk circled slowly above me, and at the edge of the parking lot, three skinny coyotes paused, observed, and then trotted away.

Raised at the edge of nature with moose, geese, foxes, and deer, I knew which plants I could eat, that I could dye wool from the lichen collected from tree branches, how the stars aligned.

As a child I collected animal bones—antlers, a moose skull, a deer skull, the vertebrae of a bear. Nature moved me then, and it moves me now, and that afternoon, the hawk and coyotes comforted me.

I wrote in my journal:

"For ladies," she's told by the doctor, "athletics promotes excessive muscular development, depleting nerve essences."

She likes to run. She's good. She's had seven miscarriages.

"But why," she asks, crossing her arms at her chest, "do long hours devoted to housework, and the care of parents, husbands, and children involve no risk?"

He chuckles but it's not mirthful. He moves across the room, opens her chart. What does this doctor look like? Let's say he has tufts of black-gray hair coming from his ears. Glasses. Plump and satisfied and distinguished. A gold pocket watch with a chain that he touches for comfort. He looks like her father and the four doctors she's been to and her husband. Like that.

"Are you saying," she continues, "that pedaling a sewing machine is all the exercise I need?"

She wears a robe over her slip. Her feet dangle from the examination table, but she sits straight.

He continues to read her chart. "Women's natural sympathies," he says, "shouldn't be replaced by assertiveness and competitiveness. Muscular achievement will outpace moral development, and the pure qualities of women's natural expression will give way to Amazonian qualities."

Athletics make you too ugly to get a husband. She's heard this before, but she's married now and it doesn't frighten her. In fact, it appeals. To become an Amazon!

She's read the latest articles, one claiming, among other things, that athletics arouses undue stimulation in females. Once stimulated, women's sexual energies will exceed the bounds of intervention and control. What then?

"Women are physically and intellectually vulnerable," he says, and she knows that this is code for inferior. "Facts," he continues. "Don't blame me. Smaller brains, lighter bones." As if to make up for everything, he adds, "You're our moral superiors. Natural models of sexual and moral virtue."

She knows that this means women are more blameworthy when they fail. When she fails.

"To jeopardize your God-given capacity to bear children," he says, "by straining your body, well, it defies both common sense and divine decree."

She looks down. Her heart opens and clenches, opens and clenches.

She folds her hands in her lap. Tears slide. Her spine curves, body caving. Soon, her cheeks are wet.

"To fulfill your destiny as a mother," he says, and she feels him looking at her, even though she's still gazing at her hands, "you're expected to monitor your activities in light of possible dangers to your reproductive functions. Overdeveloped arms and legs rob the reproductive system of vital force." He pauses. "Failure to do so," he says, "constitutes a failure to fulfill your religious, moral, and wifely duties."

She doesn't respond, and for a long moment, they listen to her crying.

"Motherhood," he says, "as you well know, is the most sacred trust the Almighty can bestow."

She's not thinking, not remembering the female athletes with six, seven, eight children. A space opens in her chest and sorrow bleeds.

"All that running," he says, "does often lead to displaced uteri."

I crossed the passage with ink, embarrassed by its maudlin tone. Then I found some old notes for an article about marathon women walkers—peds—in the late 1800s:

Walking was approved and encouraged—women forming "walking clubs"—no coaches, no unusual physical exertion, not considered "masculine," no rules, no equipment, no provocative clothing.

Lulu Loomers walked over 700 miles in 1878. Ada Anderson walked a quarter of a mile every fifteen minutes for a month. The majority of spectators women, fascinated by women performing a feat of which the majority of men incapable. Watch for hours and hours and days and days, unbridled interest.

Ada Anderson told the ladies that she hoped she was an example and that they would walk more and depend less on horse cars.

From the *Toronto Gazette*, April 12, 1879, detailing a walking match:

They were a queer lot. Tall and short, heavy and slim, young and middle-aged, some pretty and a few almost ugly . . .

The struggle in the early part of the last days was between a young woman and middle-aged Mrs. Wallace. The girl sixteen developed a great endurance and pluck. She gained gradually on her opponent, who vainly endeavored to shake her off, until, at about 4 AM, she passed Wallace. Then there were signs of war, and nearly a collision as the rivals labored . . . Wallace said something spiteful, being worked almost to a frenzy.

I read a clipping from *The New York Times* dated July 6, 1886, describing a race of 220 yards for women:

The race excited immense enthusiasm, and the ropes were broken down in several places by the eagerness of the

crowd to get a good view. There were nine starters, and
prettier girls could not have been found in the whole park.
They started off splendidly at the pistol shot, and for half
a minute there was continuous applause and excitement.
Miss Bessie Edwards led all the way, but somehow just as
the tape was reached, Miss Kate McDonald was found at
her side, and a tie was declared for the first two places, with
Miss Lily Fleming third. Misses Edwards and McDonald
went again over the course and each tried her best to win
the silver dinner service. Miss Edwards got to the tape two
yards ahead.

And another clipping from the *Toronto Gazette* on January 26, 1895:

There are some queer results of the invasion by young
women of the athletic field. Eligible bachelors are select-
ing their wives from among this class. Physical strength in
a woman attracts rather than frightens men. Some people
think that a girl's capacity to ride thirty miles on a bicycle,
to swing clubs and to punch a bag makes her strong minded;
that muscle makes her masculine and lung power loqua-
cious. This has been found to be a mistake. The up-to-date
athletic girl who patronizes the gymnasiums that are now
numerous and fashionable is not a blue stocking, although
her stockings are often blue. She is essentially feminine. She
does not as a rule want to vote, and the desire to command
or govern, except in her own province, is furthest from her
thoughts.

A poem by Edna St. Vincent Millay:

Witch-Wife

She is neither pink nor pale,
And she never will be all mine:
She learned her hand in a fairy-tale,
And her mouth on a Valentine.

She has more hair than she needs;
In the sun 'tis a woe to me!
And her voice is a string of coloured beads,
Or steps leading into the sea.

She loves me all that she can,
And her ways to my ways resign;
But she was not made for any man,
And she never will be all mine.

I wrote more:

> *Wallace and I have had many discussions about sports.*
> *"Athletes," he once told me, "are compelling because they*
> *embody achievement and competitive superiority. Darwin's*
> *theory of evolution manifest with irrefutable data, whereas*
> *it's impossible to qualify the best wife, husband, doctor,*
> *lawyer, tax accountant. Athletes embody truth."*
> *"Like poetry," I said. "Abstractions become tangible:*
> *grace, control, power, beauty."*
> *"Yes," he said. "The spirit brought to earth. There's part*
> *angel in the best athletes." He laughed then. "They can be so*
> *ignorant and dull."*

"Unappreciative," I agreed, and then, "Profundity does not an athlete make."

This was the same year my body fell apart. I'd followed the doctors' orders and became prone to bizarre accidents and injuries, even inside the supposedly safe confines of our house: stubbing my toe against a wall; bumping into a door and blackening my eye; rolling off the bed during a nightmare and snapping my radius; flipping a pot of boiled water, burning my forearm.

Outside the house, more of the same: choking on a crouton at a restaurant, my face contorting until my companion thumped my back and the food left me, clearing my airway; bit by a friend's French poodle, after she swore the dog's friendliness.

My confidence plummeted and then I gave up and the accidents stopped. No more trying to get pregnant and then bleeding it away. That earlier youthful mastery of my body, which at my best felt like a communion with the gods, an immortal feeling, had succumbed to a great physical uncertainty.

I learned the far more important and less alluring lesson that I was not in control, and that everything around me—and especially me—was fragile and impermanent. Losing because of powers beyond my control was like death, and then I had to go on living, and that's what I'm doing.

Then I closed my eyes and napped.

Jack was full of apologies on the drive back, saying that the worst part was that he knew I would've played golf better than Mr. Smith, whose swing was as stiff as a broom. His cheeks and nose were flushed and his lips chapped from the sun and wind. We had Mr. Smith's blessing now, and Flo would be joining the team in Amsterdam. We stopped and ate at a coffee shop, and

Jack tipped his flask in his coffee, adding some to mine as well. He struck a match and lit a cigarette, but I declined when he offered me one. My stomach was churned up, knowing that we were about to meet with Wallace. I tried to eat my meatloaf. Jack ate scrambled eggs, covering them in hot sauce. He would eat and drink just about anything. He was curious about how I'd spent my time in the Cadillac, and why I hadn't gone inside the clubhouse. I said that I'd used the time to think and write, and he went quiet. He was still suffering with guilt since he'd been the one to want me to come golfing in the first place. I excused myself to the restroom for the third time, and he asked if I had the nerves. After the look I gave him, he went quiet again.

Driving through the city made me thoughtful. Jack was full of questions and brimming with things he wanted to share but he left me alone. I leaned my cheek against the cool of my window, letting my breath fog it. I remembered how my mother said I was running from the time I was born. She'd send me to the store and I'd run instead of walk. No tightness in my lungs, the ground beneath me disappearing and reappearing new. A self-assuredness similar to what the whiskey brought me at its very best. At picnics, I'd beat the boys in races. Before I'd take off, I'd feel like I was in a dream, weightless. But then my weight would come behind my knees, down to my feet and into the earth, and the pistol shot or the man yelling on your mark, get set, go, would explode through me, and I'd go weightless again, flying, my arms up and down and the world quiet, passing the boys in a blur.

The remembering made me thirsty, so I reached beneath my dress and unhinged my flask from my garter. The whiskey fought with my nerves in an explosion, and my face must have shown it, because Jack said, "Easy, now." I worried that I might have to ask him to stop, unless I wanted to soil his Cadillac. But then the nausea passed, and I set my head against the window again. I started talking, surprising myself as much as Jack, who stayed very quiet, not even nodding his head.

I told him about Stamata Revithi, a thirty-year-old Greek woman, the first unofficial female Olympian. Determined to run the inaugural 40-kilometre marathon in the first Games in Athens, she left her hometown, on foot, traveling with her seventeen-month-old son strapped to her back. Ridiculed and barred, she decided to run anyway, a day after, in protest. She finished about five and a half hours later, drenched in sweat, covered in dust, and panting. Police denied her access inside the stadium, so she ran one angry lap around the perimeter.

I told him that at my high school, there were no competitive sports for girls. I sat in the stands after school each afternoon and watched the boys run track. One afternoon, the coach asked me why I was there. I told him that I wanted to run. He invited me to run a 400-metres with the boys. He thought it would be funny. In my long gym bloomers, a blouse, and black cotton stockings, I beat the entire boys' team.

"The captain," I said, "was the only one to come over and talk to me after. He wanted to find out who I was and how I could have beat them."

Jack waited for me to keep talking but I was done. He waited some more until he couldn't take it, and then he said, "And?" I remained silent, and he said, "That's not right, Mel. Finish your story."

I turned to face him. He was looking at the road but he acknowledged my stare with a nod.

"Dr. W. R. Ross," I said.

"That's how you met?"

I said nothing.

He shook his head and said, "Captain of the boys' track team. Of all things. That's quite a love story, Mel."

"It is," I agreed, and that shut him up.

We went down my street and I said, "That one," nodding at my house. Jack parked, saying, "You go. I'll wait."

"What if he doesn't want to see me?"

"He will. He agreed."

I got out of the car, went to the gate, and started up the walk. The sky was dark, almost black, the new moon giving little light. Then I heard Jack coughing in the Cadillac, and I knew that he'd taken a slug from his flask. I went back and told him to keep the noise down, and he gave me a patient look, knowing that this had nothing to do with my return. He'd already lit a cigarette. The end fired and glowed as he sucked. He held it through the opened window for me, and I took a long drag. The smoke left my mouth in a puff of white. We stayed that way—passing the flask and cigarette back and forth through his opened window—until Jack looked at his watch and said, "You're fifteen minutes late now." So I left, walking back through the gate and up the walk to the front door.

I knocked softly even though I had a key. I hadn't been home in over a month and it was improper to barge inside. I knocked again—louder—then looked through the glass at the door. His study door opened off the hall, and then a light came on. A guilty, sad pang went through me when I saw his bulky form. He was coming toward the front door, stroking the chain of his pocket watch, and another pang went through me. I pulled my face from the glass before he saw it. He didn't bother asking who it was, opening the door calmly.

I said, "Good evening, Wallace."

He stood there blinking into the dark. I wondered if he'd been drinking. Then he put his hands out and I came to him for an embrace, smelling the Scotch. When he pulled away, he looked glad to see me but then he was sad again.

He gave a long deep look into the night.

I stepped inside, telling him, "Jack's in the car."

His head went back, as if he'd spotted Jack's outline, and he shut the front door behind us. The paintings in their elaborate wood frames, the lamps, and the wallpaper were as familiar to me as my own body. But I'd pushed them from my mind, along with everything, so that their reappearance was startling.

"It's just," I began talking, not knowing what I'd say, "I'm leaving for Amsterdam. I want your blessing. But I'm leaving no matter what." I went on like this, telling him my reasons, and he watched me steadily.

When he was sure I was done, he said, "Get Jack." I was confused until he added, "I can't talk sense into you." We hadn't fought in the past and he wasn't about to start now.

So I went outside. Jack's head was leaned back against his seat, eyes closed, mouth opened, a cigarette smoldering between his fingers. I rapped my knuckles against the window, and he shot forward, almost burning his thigh. He rolled his window down farther.

"He wants to reason with you," I said, and he fumbled, mashing his cigarette in the car's ashtray, gathering his hat. He followed me inside as if I were leading him to a funeral.

We found Wallace in his study, waiting behind his desk. There was an open bottle of Scotch and an empty glass. As we entered, he didn't stand, but stayed slumped in his red-leather chair, the room smelling musty with books and Scotch. I could tell right then that he'd given up on keeping me home. He knew that I would go whether he permitted me to or not, but he would make Jack beg for it.

Jack took his hat off his head and stepped forward, saying, "She's made her decision. It has nothing to do with me."

Wallace gave no response, as if he hadn't heard.

Jack was looking at me now. "She's made her decision," he repeated. "It has nothing to do with me." His hat was going from hand to hand as if it were a ball.

Wallace slanted his eyes. "I don't know what you're insinuating, sir," he said, and then he turned to me. "Do you wish to elaborate?"

"No," I said, brusquely. I let him know with my look that I wasn't involved with Jack. Wallace eyed me. I saw that he believed me but that he still wanted to punish Jack.

Jack went into his best sales pitch then, telling Wallace that the team needed me to chaperone. History would be made, and I'd get a chance to participate. It would reflect well on Wallace. He talked about the girls, explaining their strengths. He said we had a chance to beat the United States, even with their twelve girls stacked against our four, based on our talent. The British team had been favored, but they were boycotting in protest of the limited track and field schedule. We'd come back victors and change the Olympics. He half-raised his hands and shook them as if in halfhearted victory, the pits of his shirt wet.

Wallace gave no reaction.

Jack sat in a chair in defeat. He glanced at all the leather-bound books in the bookshelf, which reached the ceiling. I'd spent hours in there, reading by myself, a small fire going in the fireplace, logs crackling.

No one spoke, and the grandfather clock in the corner ticked. Some of Wallace's old trophies were on the mantle, and a gun rack was on the opposite wall. I'd posed with each of those guns, watching my reflection in the big gilt-framed mirror by the fireplace, when no one was looking.

I wanted to tell Wallace that if I went to Amsterdam, I might return how he wanted me: All-Wife. I was sorry for not giving him children, and that sorrow coursed through everything. I loved him but I couldn't understand the love because I loved him most when I was away from him.

Wallace was thinking things he couldn't say as well. His red hair had thinned and he'd gained more weight. He always favored ice cream in grief.

Jack stood and made his way to the door. He laid his hand on the doorknob and opened it. Without looking back he said, "This dispute has nothing to do with me"—he placed his hat on his head—"and it has nothing to do with Amsterdam." He paused, as if debating whether to throw a look back at us. He didn't. "We should be going, Mrs. Ross," he said to the hall. "The girls need you." Before I could respond, he closed the door behind him.

We were quiet and then Wallace said, "Ex-wife, three kids. Two affairs that I know of."

He didn't need to tell me about Jack's unsavory background, and I took this as a cue to leave. I had made it to the door when he said, "Why do you think he helps girls? You think he's doing it because he's a good man?" He laughed, shifting in his chair. "I'll tell you why," he said. "I'll tell you why."

A few tears started but I was able to stop them, getting angry instead, thinking, Why do men always make it about them? I went out the door, down the hall—passing my fingertips across our furniture, remembering and leaving everything at once—and when I got to the front door, I wanted to slam it behind me.

I had my grip, ready to let the door fly, but then I thought about Wallace alone in our house, mixing his Scotch and water (he rarely imbibed), and I settled for shutting the door gently.

Back in the Cadillac, we headed to the house near the Athletic Club where the girls were waiting, and the sky seemed even darker than before, if possible, and packed with stars. A mist had collected at the road, and our headlights glowed through it, dipping and swerving.

Jack opened his flask and we passed it between us, steadying our nerves. But there wasn't much whiskey left, and our adrenaline from the encounter had sobered us. I had a feeling of freedom mixed with tremendous sadness, and I couldn't ever remember feeling that way before.

After some time passed Jack said, "He doesn't like me."

"He thinks," I said, "that you help the girls so that you can see them in their revealing uniforms. Running, jumping, throwing. Their thighs and arms right there for you to gape at."

He sighed and said, "Well, who wouldn't want to see them, Mel. They're beautiful."

Chapter Three
Beauty Contest

———◆———

In November 1927, I met Bonnie Brody while on assignment for the *Toronto Daily News*, sent to her small hometown of Elnora, Manitoba, for a personality piece. My editor called it a "weeper." "Tragedy Strikes Family of Champion Athlete" ran the headline. Bonnie and her family had buried her mother three months earlier.

Bonnie, like the other girls on our Olympic team, was an all-rounder, great at a variety of sports, and Bonnie's mother liked to walk her to her afternoon high school basketball practices.

It was one of those ideal afternoons—warm and pleasant with a cool breeze, shadows of clouds skimming the grass—that seem retrospectively fated by its perfection.

Mother and Daughter said a casual good-bye, turning to go their separate ways.

Bonnie didn't see the Model T's wild swerve at the corner of Jeffers and Pillsbury. But she heard the screeches and screams, and she ran to find her mother lying bloody and broken on the street.

Coach Frank, the boys' baseball coach, ran from the field, and he stayed with Bonnie through the ambulance ride and at the hospital, until her own father arrived hours later, due to his being out of town on business.

At the hospital, Bonnie yelled for her mother long after the nurse pulled a sheet over Mrs. Brody's head and declared her dead. Three nurses and Coach Frank held Bonnie while a doctor sedated her with an injection.

When her drug-fog lifted, her screams switched to an existential grievance that I've often pondered: "Who's in charge? Tell me who's in charge!" and the nurses and Coach Frank held her for the doctor's repeat injection.

Much like reading necessitates the reader's participation, hearing the accident charged Bonnie's imagination.

She relived the crash in detail, over and over, as if inside of it. An insatiable drive and anger overtook her, ostracizing her father and six siblings. Wanting to help, Coach Frank began training her for the Olympic 100-metres. Want, need, and grief blazed through her feet, and she ran and ran and hurt and ran.

Her father remarried, and while the town was forgiving—he needed help raising those kids—his firstborn daughter was not.

She latched onto Coach Frank. Almost twice her sixteen-year age, he was married with two kids and one on the way. Their relationship was unconventional, as was Coach Frank's regimen: he drove his car alongside his sprinting protégée, yelling directions out the window, and every afternoon, she ran the bases with the boys' baseball team.

Townsfolk witnessed on more than one occasion their private, intimate embraces. But despite the whisperings, Elnora believed in Bonnie and sponsored her with numerous food drives and fund-raisers.

The winters in Elnora can be rough and frozen, and Elnora was especially durable in response: frugal, religious, rigid, conservative. Populated mainly with Scottish immigrants, Elnora prayed for prosperity, health, peace, and for Bonnie Brody to win gold. God had summoned Bonnie. Even her mother's death, they told her, was a thread in a divine tapestry. Guarded and suspicious, Bonnie nonetheless fell sway to Elnora's worship of her.

At night—every night—she looked in her mirror, said to her reflection 125 times: "Hello, Bonnie Brody, gold-medal winner."

Having set a world record at the Canadian Women's Track and Field Championship and surpassing it to set another at the qualifications, she (100-metres) and Ginger (high jump) were the expectant gold-winners.

The papers thrived on her tragedy for a while and then focused once more on the Dream Girl this, the Dream Girl that. Everywhere Bonnie looked: Dream Girl photographs and articles.

The week before our train was to leave, Bonnie came to stay at the house in Toronto, rooming with Flo. Bonnie had turned seventeen the month before, and Flo was three months her elder.

Her second afternoon, I was reading the newspaper at the kitchen table, and Bonnie walked in and looked down at me, her eyes an inky pained blue.

I needed to talk to her, had promised Jack that I would, and was sorting out how to do so. She wore a denim skirt with pockets, gym socks pulled to her knees, and flat oxfords. Her hair was cut in the Eton style, slicked and bangs plastered. But her hair constantly fought back, wild and angry.

Pulling a chair from the table, she said, "Can I tell you something?" and then she sat. She hesitated, and then asked, "Why does she get all the attention?"

"Who?" I asked, even though I knew.

"I don't care if she's so pretty," she said.

"They do."

"Stupid," she said, and rolled her eyes.

"The press doesn't care what we think."

"It's not a beauty pageant," she said.

"We've been hearing," I said, "how women athletes have beards and hair on their chests, and now they have someone they can't take their eyes off."

"It's awful," she said.

"I know."

"Isn't there some way to change it?" she asked. "She's letting it go to her head."

I didn't agree and said, "It confuses her."

For a moment, she acted as if she hadn't heard me, and then she said, "She's a stupid sap." That was the last thing I wanted to hear. "She's a sap," she said again, and as I looked at her face, I saw something ugly and mean under the grief, as though hiding behind a mask. "Acting like a little girl," she continued, "with that ukulele and doll." She was talking about the ukulele and rag doll that Ginger kept on her bed. The rag doll was hand-stitched with an embroidered face and the ukulele was made of dark wood. Ginger acted like they were treasure.

I was going to tell Bonnie that I had the power to pull her from the team, even if I wasn't sure that I did. But I settled for, "We're a team."

She mumbled something I couldn't hear. Then she said, "I want to win so bad, Mel, I lay awake at night wanting." Her voice was mournful, her hands on her knees. "I lie there all night wanting. I have to win. I go sick from it. It's inside me and"—she leaned back—"What if I don't win, Mel?" she said. "What then?"

I was going to quote de Coubertin's motto: *The important thing in the Olympic Games is not to win but to take part; the important thing in life is not the triumph but the struggle.* But it struck me as disingenuous and I said nothing.

She stood from her chair and said, "I'm favored."

"Sure," I said, because it was true.

"That's not a guarantee."

"No," I agreed. "It's not."

She was waiting for more but I was in no mood to appease.

Bonnie looked at me expectantly, her hands at the back of her chair.

"Everyone wants to win," I said. "It's no secret. What makes you different? You think God's got you picked out? You think the world owes you?"

She looked at me, giving me a full-shock stare.

"I was eight," I said, "when my mom died."

That got her to sit again.

"You lose," I said, "and life goes on."

"I don't know," she said, shaking her head. "I don't know if mine will. I'll die."

I was going to try to explain that she could learn about life from losing. That defeat was bitter, but that you have to analyze a loss. But just then, Flo came in, giving us a scanning look. "What're you talking about?" she asked.

"Nothing," Bonnie said.

Flo sensed the weight in the room. She hated school, got poor grades, but she was one of those athletes who excelled at playing head games with her opponents, so I was never sure if she was as simpleminded as she acted. She was our 800-metres girl, trained for the long run, so I knew she had some depth.

"Come on," Flo said.

I didn't answer and Bonnie said nothing.

Flo pulled a chair and sat next to Bonnie to prove that she wasn't going anywhere. She wore a low-waisted blue dress, the shapeless popular kind that looked best on skinny girls with small breasts and no hips. She looked like a twelve-year-old boy, especially with her short hair, but she wore dark red lipstick, and a flower clip pulled back her bangs.

"Mel was talking about God and country," Bonnie said.

"What about it?" Flo asked.

Bonnie believed she was clever and didn't expect me to answer. But I thought about it a moment and responded. I told them that most of us believed that God wanted us to win, not our opponents. God favored us. Our country. But that deep down, each of us knew that this wasn't really true, and that it didn't really matter.

"How can you say that?" Bonnie said.

"Before I run," Flo said, looking very serious, "I tap my left thigh three times with my right hand and my right thigh four times with my left hand, real fast so no one notices." She paused, and then she demonstrated.

"If I don't," she said, "I'm afraid I'll lose."

We were quiet for a bit and then Bonnie said, "I have to wear the same underwear."

Flo pinched her nostrils and said, "P.U."

"I wash them!" said Bonnie. "Actually they wore out. So I cut patches and sewed them on my others."

"For God and country," said Flo, and we laughed.

"I raced this girl," said Bonnie, "who told me before our race that Christ was on her side."

"What happened?" I asked.

"I got the biggest kick out of beating her."

We laughed again. Then Bonnie said that even when she was watching others compete, she'd sometimes hold her breath and close her eyes, as if the outcome depended on her. Flo said that when she was a girl, she used to believe that the whole world issued from her, like photographs from her mind projected outward.

"Then you grew up," said Bonnie.

"I guess so," said Flo, and then she said that she still felt that way when she won a race. "There's this thing inside me," she said, "that doesn't want to be the same as everyone else."

"I always have this dream," Bonnie said, "that I'm running and my feet fall off."

Right around that time, Jack knocked on the door and I yelled for him to come in. "Hello," he said, giving us the once-over. He reached into his jacket and pulled out his cigarette case. I thought he might offer me one but he decided against it.

"Where are the sisters?" he asked, tapping a cigarette against his palm. He set the cigarette in his mouth.

I wanted to tell him that he was an awful example, but I was just angry because I couldn't smoke in front of the girls.

"They went for a walk," I said, letting him know by my voice how I felt about the inequality. But he ignored me.

He was on his way to lighting the cigarette when he looked at Bonnie, looked at me, and said, "So you told her."

"Oh, Jack," I said.

He shook out his match.

"Told me what?" said Bonnie.

"Nothing, honey," said Jack, realizing his mistake.

"Told me what?" Bonnie said, looking at me. I, in turn, looked back at Jack. He'd been relying on me to tell her, but now it had become his job. I made sure to make that clear with my facial expression.

"Ah, Jesus, Mel," he said, by way of acknowledgement.

Flo was taking everything in with her big-eyed stare but I gave her a nod. "Can't I stay?" she asked, and she got her answer with Jack's grim face. She stood up and left the kitchen.

Jack took his place in her chair. He pulled off his hat and set it on the table. Smoke came from the side of his mouth.

"What?" said Bonnie. "Told me what?"

Jack didn't answer, his head hanging. Then he stubbed his cigarette in our tin ashtray and gave her a long and sorry look. "Coach Frank," he said, "will not be joining us in Amsterdam."

He watched her. She was staring back at him, but then she looked down.

"I'm sorry, honey. It's not in the cards."

Her face came up with a startling angry intensity. Her eyes glittered and she leaned toward him. "I won't go," she said. "I won't go without him."

Jack said nothing and she waited. She waited and she kept staring at him and he stared back at her without a word.

Then he said, "You're a quitter."

"What?" she said. "Are you kidding?" Her mouth twisted and she mimicked him in a nasty voice—"You're a quitter." She laughed mean and artificial. "Is that all you can say? This is all about money. It's always about money. I'm not going if he doesn't."

Jack looked at me, shook his head sadly, and then said, "A familiar story. Quits because of a man. I've heard it a million times before, Mel."

He sighed, still looking at me. "Coach Frank," he said, "and his wife have a baby coming. His wife's not so keen on him traveling. Seems understandable, wouldn't you agree, Mel?"

I said that I would.

"Have you met his wife?" he asked.

I said that I hadn't but that I'd heard that she was delightful.

"She feels very strongly," he said, "that Coach Frank stay home."

I said that I had heard about this development and that it made sense.

"Did you know," he said to me, "that there's been some nasty rumors?"

I said that I did my best to ignore malicious gossip.

"Good girl," he said, solemn. He paused, asked, "You know a thing or two about running the hundred metres, Mel?"

I said that I did.

"You'd be willing to impart this information?"

I said that I'd coach to the best of my ability along with Coach Sacks. That as I saw it, my duty was to the girls: to chaperone them, dispense advice and sympathy, and buffer them from Jack's ego and domineering behavior.

"You're a peach, Mel," he said, ignoring my insults. He gave me a full-on Jack smile. "Has anyone told you that?"

I said that he had.

Bonnie had been watching us with a blank amazement, but now her face looked as though she might scream or cry or both at once. But she remained silent, her hands splayed on the table, and her breathing thickened.

I placed my hand on her forearm. She shook it off, setting her palms to her eyes, fingers at her forehead, as if to hold in her brain. "I can't run," she said. "I need him. I can't win without him." She shook her head, and her hands stayed at her face.

"You think you need him but you don't," I said, and I believed this. "He's your coach. He's not you."

"That's right, honey," Jack murmured. "That's right. You don't need Coach Frank. You've got everything you need inside of you."

She released her hands, the skin around her eyes flushed. There was a long and heavy silence where we all went back and forth looking at each other.

Then Jack stood, took his hat from the table. He said, "I'm no good at this." He had his hat in front of his stomach in both hands as if he were at church, and the sweat showed on his face.

He went to her, leaned in and whispered in her ear. He kept on whispering, and her head lowered. After he left, she still wouldn't let the tears come. I sat with her because she asked me to stay. I wanted to know what Jack had told her but I didn't ask.

Chapter Four
Farmer

I woke one morning with a hangover, no one in the house, my head buzzing. The girls were at practice. Drinking a glass of water, I saw Ginger's bloomers hanging at the back of a chair, her running shoes beneath. They fit. Then I found myself running out of the house's shadow into the warm sunlight, over hilly ground with grass into a flat field, and onto a packed dirt road toward the woods. The buzzing diminished and I remembered the painful, rhythmic, achy, tremendous feel of running. My stride was ungainly but I enjoyed eating up the ground with my feet. Breathing hard, I endured and my lungs pounded. The smell was clean and healthy, the air sweet. Overhead, the tree branches canopied and cut the sun. I lengthened my stride to get a pain out of my side, and it worked all right. I was conscious of the heat and my sweat, and a curious giddiness came over me, as though I were charged with electricity. I'm not sure how long I was out there, but I ran to a steady jog-trot rhythm, and then it was so smooth I forgot I was running. I was hardly able to know that my legs were lifting and falling and my arms going in and out. My heart had gone from thumping in my temples to a steady thrum. I didn't know I was walking until the noise of a squirrel rustling inside a bush brought me back, and I had a coughing fit.

Walking home, I saw the girls to my left some distance away, tiny and bright colored, practicing with more girls. There was Coach Sacks hobbling, and I heard his whistle. Some girls lying on their backs sprang up in sit-ups; some rotated their torsos, hands at their hips; and some stretched forward, touching their toes. A pack ran around the track in one giant dot.

That evening, for the first time in months, I didn't pine for the taste of whiskey and the accompanying pleasure of nicotine. My body hurt in the best way. Instead of my usual strained appetite, I ate a generous dinner, savoring the meal. My mind was too tired to grapple with my usual insomnia, and I fell asleep quickly, without the aid of alcohol or sedatives, into a prolonged deep slumber.

After that, in the mornings when the girls practiced, I went for my secret runs. Ginger had plenty of bloomers and shoes and she let me have hers without question, not because she was polite but because she didn't care. She wasn't interested in my idiosyncrasies. No one would have supposed that a thirty-eight-year-old woman sidelined from exercising by doctors' orders had taken up a running habit. I'd thought and written a lot about running since I'd stopped, but the thinking and writing was nothing compared with the doing. The feeling of solace was worth the risk of being caught. There was something quietly spiritual for me, listening to the *hih-huh* of my breath coupled with the *tap-teck* of my feet. I was not as likely to worry about headaches, digestive troubles, insomnia, and backaches, and the discomfort (and pain) of the exertion was worth the feeling of pleasure produced at its termination. The stopping was even better than the starting.

Two mornings before we were to leave by train to Montreal, I went for a long run while the girls practiced. Muriel Ziegler, our javelin girl, had arrived at the house late the night before from Alberta and Jack had agreed that she needed her rest, excusing her from practice. She was a small-town girl, a Russian Jew, and a sports veteran at twenty-two. Quick-witted and quick-tongued, with black bobbed hair and a muscular wiry body, she was popular. The girls voted her team captain unanimously.

As a girl, whenever anyone saw her, she was running, and always very fast. "Why walk when you can run," she told a newspaper reporter later. A club-shaped scar extended from the corner of her eyelid down and across her jawline. She got it at seven from jumping off a barn roof with a crowd of children watching. She landed with a flourish, kicking up dust. Kids laughed and clapped but then silenced when she shrieked in pain, her bloody face looking up. She'd hit her head on a piece of wood, barely missing an eye. The next day, her face bruised and stitched, she performed the same stunt in front of an even larger audience, determined to get it right. She crashed just as hard, cracking two ribs.

At eight, she took up marbles, practiced for hours, until the entire neighborhood of marble-players refused to play and lose to her. At nine, she participated in baseball, hockey, and football with the boys, winning their respect. At eleven, she took on a school bully, and put up a good fight. Some said he'd won but it didn't matter. That same year, she invented a game called Train Race, but after slipping while running alongside the train, almost getting yanked beneath its wheels, she stopped. Once, she climbed a huge tree in front of her elementary school, balanced at the top. "I wanted to know what it was like," she said, "to look down on everyone." She perched there like a hawk until the principal called for her to come down or risk expulsion.

One forgets that he is watching a girl, wrote a reporter, *for there isn't the slightest semblance of anything feminine about her, or in her actions.* The press was in a debate as to whether they loved or hated her. She gave great one-liners. But she didn't even pretend to care what they thought, not bothering with lipstick or girdles. In posed photos, even when vociferously encouraged to smile, she always gave the camera a dead-on-serious-grim-faced stare. Peterson Chocolates, where she worked in the factory, was her loyal sponsor. The girls called her Farmer and the press picked it up, but she didn't mind. "It's better than the Dream Girl," she said.

Muriel was still in bed when I left. I decided to run anyway, sneak back without her knowing. The sky was gray with clouds, sun poking through. A mile or so away was the dark-green wall of woods. I ran into the field and onto the dirt road carpeted with leaves. I continued at a comfortable pace, every few steps hearing a leaf or a small branch snap under my shoes.

Then I was fully in the woods—a first—hurdling fallen logs, twisting through bramble. The earth smelled sweetly clean, the air noticeably cooled beneath the big trees.

My foot caught on a rock and I fell forward. On the ground, I spat dirt from my mouth. I knew dirt was all over my face, my cheek scraped—blood at my fingers when I touched. One of those stinging scrapes, I decided, that hurt worse than it looked.

I was up again and heading out of the woods, both angry that I'd lost my footing and invigorated by my daring at going in the woods. My mouth had gone dry and I summoned saliva and spat.

I imagined I was being followed and if I was caught I'd be killed—a game that I used to play as a girl when I ran, simply for the thrill—and quickened my pace.

Out of the woods, the gray had burned off. Birds sang and I heard the frenetic scrambling of a small animal nearby. Overhead a great flock of blackbirds rose and fell and streamed past me in a squawking rush.

Then I saw a figure walking ahead of me—light, brisk, slightly pigeon-toed. I sprang to the side but it was too late. The person waved. Farmer.

I slowed and walked to her and she walked to me. She wore bloomers, a blouse, running shoes, and a blue cloche hat. The breeze cooled me like silk. When we reached each other, she said, "Your secret's safe."

"Thanks," I said.

"Your face is dirty," she said. Before I responded, she said, "Don't say I hit you or something."

"I'll say I fell," I said. "It's true."

"A little powder," she said, squinting and tilting her head, as though imagining makeup on me. "No one will bother you." A nerve jumped beside her right eye, under her scar.

"Doctors," I said, feeling the need to explain, "told me to stop when I was younger. I took it up again by surprise."

"Doctors," she said, "slap you when you come out your momma. From there on, they want you to curl up like a bug and die."

"I'm too old," I said, "to be running." Then I corrected myself. "To be seen running."

"Once," she said, "a man saw me running and he called the police."

"Why?"

"He figured that someone was chasing me, or that I was sick. 'Girls don't run,' he said. The cops came and talked to Momma. She said, 'Oh no, she's fine. Don't worry. That's just what Muriel does.'"

"A concerned citizen," I said.

"A fine man," she agreed.

"His duty," I said.

"Women," she said, "have incredible stamina." She started walking at a quick pace, motioning for me to follow. We jogged in a concentrated silence, our legs in sync. Then she moved ahead in a sprint. I tried to keep pace but gave up and stopped, catching my breath, and watched the blue and white of her shirt, bloomers, and hat. She was so fast and beautiful. My peak was long gone, and I wished then for that wholeness to return.

It was sometime well after midnight when Farmer knocked on my bedroom door, and I slowly came to from a corpse-like sleep. I found my way to the door, opened it.

"Bonnie's drunk," she said, not wasting words.

A jolt of fear went through me, until I realized my stash was well hidden under my bed, safe from blame, and the fear turned to an alert panic.

"Where'd she get it?"

Farmer shrugged an I-don't-know. "She's hollering," she said, "about her coach."

"Hold on," I said, going for my robe.

"Sorry to wake you," Farmer said. "I've been up with her, trying to take care. But it's getting worse."

I looked out my window, confirming that it was a deep-dark-everyone-asleep outside.

Pretending to need my slippers, I kneeled and looked under my bed, reached my hand and felt my flask and bottle, tested their weight. Secure.

I followed Farmer toward Flo and Bonnie's bedroom. There was a sound coming from inside, reminding me of cats mating.

"I'm not paid enough," I said to no one.

The sisters stood in the hallway near their bedroom, wide-eyed, identical nightgowns, hands clutched across their torsos. They even had their heads tilted the same. The only difference was that Ginger had her rag doll.

"Go on back to sleep," I said.

They didn't move.

"Go on!" I said.

"Go on," Farmer said, far more gentle, "go on, everything's okay. Don't worry, everything's okay."

They followed Farmer's instruction, throwing cautious looks back at us.

I made to knock at the door of the bedroom but Farmer opened it and we went inside. The light was on, and Bonnie sat on her bed, hands crossed at her chest. She was catching her breath to make more noise. Flo sat next to her and turned her head to us when we entered. Bonnie's head didn't turn. Her mouth opened and her tongue came out. She made her cat noise, and Flo shushed her.

Bonnie shook her head violently. "I love him," she said, and Flo said, "I know, I know," and Farmer came to the bed, saying, "Everything's going to be okay."

"Where'd she get it?" I asked Flo, searching the room, and Flo swore up and down and on her mother's life and her father's and brothers' and even her beloved dog's that she didn't know a thing.

"Come here," I said, and I made Flo breathe into my face. The whole room smelled of gin and I couldn't tell one way or the other. I interrogated her more and then lost heart. "Go to the sisters'," I told her. "Take your pillow and covers, get some sleep. We've got a train to catch in the morning."

Flo nodded, grabbed her things, and then she was gone, closing the door quiet behind her.

The shrieking went on for about an hour and then Bonnie's face started changing colors. I told Farmer to get the bucket from the kitchen. She was fast and came back in time with two, placing one between Bonnie's feet. She tucked Bonnie's hair behind her ears and adjusted her head.

I searched again for a bottle, hoping to get an idea of what we were dealing with, and all the time I was looking, there was a horrible retching noise—silence—retching—silence, and finally a soft moaning. It smelled like an acidic combination of gin, corn, and mashed potatoes, in remembrance of our dinner.

Farmer went to empty the buckets, and I arranged Bonnie in her bed, tucking her in like a little girl, the cover tight under her chin. She was snoring with her mouth wide open by the time Farmer returned.

"Better stay," Farmer said, and I agreed. Farmer turned off the light and tucked in beside Bonnie, and I fell asleep at Flo's bed.

Before long, the sun shined through the window, and when I opened my eyes, Farmer was staring from her bed at me, as if she'd just opened her eyes, saying, "Good morning, Mel."

"Morning, Farmer."

We sat up and conversed a bit, and soon Bonnie sat up, testing her lips and mouth with her tongue. Pale and horrified, her eyes going from me to Farmer then to the wall, she said, "I got drunk."

"Sure did," I said.

"I never did before," she said, her eyes making their rounds again. "I never even took a sip before." Incredulous, and then she seemed to understand that she was in serious trouble because she went into a meditation without further commentary.

After some time passed, Farmer asked, "You okay?"

Bonnie shifted, as if testing her insides. She moved her arms and legs, swallowed a few times. "I think I'm all right," she said. She looked at me with frightful eyes, took another swallow. "I'm all right," she said, and then, "I'm so thirsty."

"You're dehydrated," I said.

"That's what happens," said Farmer.

"Where'd you get it?" I asked, and I never did find out who gave her the liquor and still wonder to this day.

She shot me a sickened look, and then padded her way to the bathroom. We heard her drinking from the faucet. Then the noise changed to coughing. When that was done, she was at the doorway again, leaned against it, and she said miserably, "I feel so sick. My head hurts."

"That's what happens," I said, but she wasn't listening, gulping from the faucet again. After that, she did a crouch-walk back to the bed, sat gingerly, and cradled her head in her hands.

"Was he worth it?" I asked.

Her head came up and she seemed to ponder the question.

Farmer said, "Leave her be, Mel." But then she looked at Bonnie, adding, "Well, was he?"

"No," Bonnie said, but I got the impression that the breadth of her love for Coach Frank impressed her.

Chapter Five

Slip Aways

Late that morning, with the train pitching us forward into the bright day, puffing across its track, and after the girls had gone wild over their seats that converted into sleeping compartments, instigating an impromptu pillow fight, I sat in the lounge compartment across from Jack and said to him, "The Peerless Four. The papers are calling the girls the Peerless Four."

He smoked his cigarette and observed me, his body rocking gently with the train's movement. "Can you believe that crowd?" he asked. There'd been a brass band and a preacher offering up prayers. At least five hundred well-wishers. Flags, banners, confetti, a speech from the mayor.

Jack had yelled at the girls because Coach Sacks didn't believe in yelling, after they'd already been shouted at for their pillow fight, chastising them for drinking soda and—"yes, that's right, at least one of you that I know of was caught drunk last night, that's right, drunk!"—the girls listening with bowed heads. Now there was a pleasant, chastened quiet.

"I love trains," Jack said. "I always feel like I'm getting away with something when I'm on one." He smiled, his head pivoting to make sure no one was watching, passed me his smoke.

"Like running away from home," he said, spotting Flo and Bonnie and snatching his cigarette back before I got a hold of it in my lips.

The train let out a whistle and he said, "Best sound in the world, lonely and happy all at once." He contemplated me some more. "You know what that feels like, don't you?" In case I'd missed his insinuation, he added, "Lonely and happy. You know what it feels like to run away from home, Mel?"

I said that I did and I asked him to shut up.

His eyes went to the window and the blur of sun and landscape. "The Peerless Four," he said to the window. He nodded. "Yes," he said. "I like it."

He closed his eyes, his chin going down, and lapsed into a nap, causing a coil of jealousy to rise inside me. I could no sooner sleep in public then eat my own fist. His cigarette smoldered between his knuckled fingers, his hand at his knee. I took the smoke and finished it in four long and satisfying pulls, looking around as I did so as to make sure no one noticed. Then I watched Jack's chin tremble at his sternum. Every now and then, he lurched, his eyelids lifting. But then he righted himself and was off slumbering again.

I pulled a novel from my purse. Always, I had a book to read. As a girl, reading was central to my development. No one else would teach me what I wanted to know. I sneaked books that I wasn't allowed to read, and when I became an adult, I read them in the open. I read to become wiser and then I read more because I wasn't any wiser, and then more still. I read to find out what it was like to be a man. To be Russian, Spanish, and French, to be a different race, to be royalty, dirt-poor, a wealthy New Yorker, a

homesteader or a gold miner in the pioneer West. I read for pleasure, distraction, sustenance, enlightenment, instruction, and to
pass the time. I read the Bible because I was supposed to learn
about God and Jesus and loving my neighbor and an eye for an
eye and turn the other cheek. But the more I read the Bible, the
more confused I was. So I read to find out about the universe,
to discover how sex worked, how babies were born, what was
moral, what was immoral. How to live. I read to find out what it
was like in another's skin. Did other people doubt, feel, and fear
like me? If not, why? What was I missing? What did they know
that I did not?

So, there on the train, I opened my book, which happened to
be Edith Wharton's *House of Mirth*. But after about five minutes,
my attention strayed to Jack, staring at his hands, resting and
vibrating at his knees. I thought about how we met, which was
my lying to him, telling him the paper had sent me to write a
profile. In truth I was done with the paper by then, tired of all the
myth-making fabrications, of being directed to write about female
athletes' clothes and shopping habits rather than their skills, not
wanting to be a part of the Giant Lie.

I was in one of my worst prolonged Slip Aways—not like my
childhood Slip Aways—a bad one, sleeping late and then waking
to watch the day from my window. Wallace didn't bother me,
so I could lie there as long as I wanted, going over all the things
I wouldn't be doing—writing, reading, going to the moving pictures, lunching, shopping, visiting friends—letting it slide like
water off my skin. Yes, during bad Slip Aways, even reading failed
me, and the most I could do was look out the window. I'd continue lying there, deciding not to get up, floating above, around,

inside death, similar to falling asleep, drifting, and then a door slams or a thought erupts and pulls you back, and you never *die*. An aimless reverie that ends not in the void, only near it.

But this time I'd gone too far, staying in bed for days that turned into weeks, smuggling in whiskey, hiding bottles, bribing poor Patricia, our housekeeper, to collude in my deception. It had happened once before, sometime after my final miscarriage and after I'd stopped writing. I'd been working on a biography of Onata Green, a distant relative, an Iroquois female lacrosse player, and I dug a pit in the yard, burned a box of my old running shoes, so that Wallace came home to a scorched patch on our lawn and made me go see another doctor, this time for my head. The doctor was useless except for the sedatives he prescribed. The afternoon I dragged myself from bed to meet Jack, I'd been getting better, going that week to lunch with a friend, and once for a swim, and to Jack's Athletic Club to watch the girls stretch, run, play basketball, and, my favorite, badminton, the feather-like ball jerk-floating between their racket slaps.

That afternoon, he sat behind his desk and I sat in a chair before him, firing one indelicate question after another, notebook open at my lap, alluding to his ulterior motives, when he coughed, laughed, asked, "What kind of column did you say you were writing, Mrs. Ross?"

"Mel," I corrected.

"Mel," he said, trying it out. "Mel, Mel." I wore a long dress that reached my ankles, and he appeared to be studying them. His eyes lifted back to mine. "Now, Mel, what kind of article is this?"

"Why," I asked, "hire girls that don't know how to type or dictate?"

"Charity?" he said, a lilting question, asking me to accept. "Goodwill?" He paused. "I can't see your eyes," he said, "under that hat."

"Do you like muscular women?"

He grinned sourly, peered as if he could see beneath my dress, answered in deadpan: "I like all women, Mel."

My face heated and I pulled my eyes from him, collected my nerves.

He lifted from his chair, went to the water cooler at the corner of his office. When he leaned forward to fill his cone-shaped paper cup, I saw that his shirt was stuck to his back.

He slugged down about ten cups—probably hungover—before returning to his desk. He seemed to have calmed, lighting a cigarette and giving me a spiel about how his mother and sisters had been thwarted athletes. When his hockey career ended, he said, he found a new purpose.

"Why'd you stop playing?"

He smiled in a peculiar way, and then ran his tongue over his lips. His expression grew somber. "Let's see," he said. "Was it the arthritis in my hips and knees, or the constant pain in my legs?" He went on in this manner: It might have been because he kept separating his shoulder, he said, having to jam it back in its place. Maybe because he was either losing his bowels or regurgitating before each game, and sometimes both. Or the times he got beat up on the ice, fists coming at him. His third smashed nose. Or when he played with a broken arm, permanently damaging it, leaving it longer than the other.

He stood, hung both arms before his chest. A visible difference of an inch or more.

He sat again. We were quiet, and then he said that despite everything, he missed the adulation and attention. That hockey was in his blood, no matter how much he hated it, or tried to hate it. He couldn't get it out of his blood.

"Loved and worshiped," he said, smiling as if looking into a bright light, "as long as you win."

He paused to smoke and consider, then added, "What do you do, Mel, when the one thing that you truly love, the thing that you're most good at in the world, the one thing that you depended on and lived for, becomes the thing that gives you the most pain?"

His face went down and he finished his cigarette. When he was done, he stubbed it out in the ashtray at his desk.

I couldn't take his open sadness and went back to my previous tactic.

"Have you ever had a relationship," I asked, "with one of your athletes?"

He squinted at me, confused, possibly wounded.

"Hire me," I said.

He brooded over that for a long time. Then he said, "What?"

"Hire me."

"Now why," he asked, "in goddamn holy hell would I do that?"

"My husband," I said, "is Dr. W. R. Ross."

"I know who you are," he said, squinting again.

"Do you know my husband?"

"Of course."

"You'll come across better," I said.

"I'm doing okay."

"Public relations," I said. "Legitimacy. Approval."

He threw his hands up. "Christ, Mel," he said.

Though I was no bohemian, I was willing to be unconventional if it was understated and didn't cause trouble or seem indecent. Jack hired me. Wallace reluctantly agreed to let me move out temporarily to chaperone the girls as they trained, saying that he admired my devotion and unswerving dedication to furthering the cause of females in athletics.

In other words: he was relieved and expected me to shake off my depression. But then time passed and he wanted me home, and I said no. The only thing that I could fathom he needed me for was to re-button his vests, for he was in the habit of buttoning them up wrong. But Patricia could do that, along with providing his meals and turning down his bed. I couldn't breathe in our house, and at least I was breathing now, but I didn't tell him that.

I watched Jack nap and lurch and nap. I read. He woke. We talked. We ate grilled cheese sandwiches. The girls played cards and watched the countryside. Farmer read a book on relay-race technique. Bonnie and Flo hurdled over legs stretched out in the aisle until I made them stop, and then they did calisthenics and jogged in place. Ginger and Danny met a boy on the track team named Hugh Williams, and they sat and talked. But we separated the men's track team from our team after Flo was caught in a private room with a pole-vaulter.

The train got quiet again, and then we arrived at Montreal's Bonaventure Station close to midnight. Spent and tired, we listened to the mayor's speech, and then lumbered with our luggage and boarded the buses for the short ride to the pier. There we somberly transferred to the White Star Line ocean liner SS *Albertic*, which loomed like a creaking monster in its dock.

At the ship I ate two slices of buttered toast and the girls ate sandwiches and drank glasses of milk. Everyone was exhausted and nervous. I made sure the girls were safe and comfortable in their rooms, and then went to my room. This took a while. Only Farmer had been further east than Halifax, and the girls were excited and scared. There were tears and prayers and appeasements, and then I finally went to my room. I got the light turned on and a pitcher of water and a glass set up beside my bed. I took off my shoes and dress and put on my nightgown, propped myself in bed with Wharton. It had begun to drizzle outside, the rain dripping against the dark of my porthole window. The movement of the ship rocked me, blending with the earlier sensation of the train. I yawned. The words in the book floated and my eyelids began to drop.

"Mel," said Jack's voice outside my door. *Tap tap.* "Mel, open up."

For a moment I didn't answer, but he kept at it and I opened the door.

"What took you?" He wore pajama tops beneath his jacket, tucked haphazardly into his pants.

"Too tired," I said.

"Can I come in anyway?"

He looked sad and bleary, and I said okay, just for a little bit. I went to the bed, propped myself up. He came over and took a seat beside me. Really, there wasn't space to sit anywhere else.

He leaned forward, poured water into the glass from the pitcher, drank it, poured another, and offered it to me. I drank. The entire time he stared at me with a deep troubled look.

"What's eating you?" I asked, wiping water that had dribbled on my chin.

His face worked as though he was trying to say something important. Then he sank into himself and gave up.

For a long time, we listened to the rain slap at the window. There was a feeling in the room.

Then I said, "You need to go back to your room," because I had to say it.

He didn't answer. He just looked at me.

"People will talk," I said.

"They already do," he said. "Don't you know that?"

"What do they say?"

"They say that you and me"—he lifted his hand, intertwining his forefinger with his middle—"are like this."

His fingers dropped. Then his hand went to my knee and a pleading look came to his eyes.

This was the first time he'd tried anything with me. I'd been expecting this kind of visit, but it came as a surprise anyhow.

"All right," I heard my voice say, and my fingers twitched as I took his hand and set it in his lap. There was still heat on my knee, even without him touching me. It surprised me. I thought I was done with those sorts of sensations. Unseemly, I believed, for a woman my age to have notions, romance being youth's terrain. But I believed a lot of things then that I don't now.

"C'mon, Mel," he whispered, leaning into me. His breath landed at my neck and my heart went soft.

Somehow, I told him to stop.

He did and asked, "Why?"

"My reputation," I said.

"Your reputation?" he said, as if I'd given him a stupid answer.

Tears welled, making him swim out of focus for a second, and then one broke from my lash and ran down my cheek. I swiped it and no more came.

But he noticed and looked down. He said, "Sorry, Mel. I've had too much—" he lifted his flask from his pocket, shook it ceremoniously and his face stayed down. But he was using the liquor as an excuse.

"Sometimes," he'd once told me, in an inebriated and babbling condition, "in the mornings I don't want to wake up." The one thought, he said, strong enough to pull him from his bed, encouraging him to once again partake of the sweet nectar called life, was the sheer possibility of settling his face in between a woman's thighs, tasting that far more rewarding nectar.

Did he remember telling me? That was the way he was and I couldn't change him. It wasn't the perversity. I'd heard of those predilections before. I was no innocent. But I believed it didn't matter if they were my legs or someone else's. Women—not me— were his salve. This was what I believed.

He reinserted his flask in its pocket. "I'll go," he said, looking at me with a searching expression. When I didn't answer, he apologized while pulling himself to a stand. He paused at the doorway, a suffering pride settling over his features, said it wouldn't happen again, he could promise me that, and then he left.

Chapter Six

Onata Green

———◆———

Girls who went to college like me, it was widely believed, were apt to become old maids and bookworms, a dire threat to any girl's chance of attracting a husband and thus having a worthwhile life. The fear turned out to be valid. After the experience, many women decided not to marry. Instead they pursued social reforms and careers, especially withing the suffragist movement. But I was not at risk, as Wallace and I were already married when we both attended Lawrenceville University, now defunct, Wallace to pursue medicine, and me in the Department of Domestic Sciences, designed and initiated to create top-notch wives and mothers.

In admitting girls into higher education, the university was working against years of bias, including journalist, historian, and academic Henry Adams, who observed "the pathetic impossibility of improving those poor little hard, thin, wiry, one-stringed instruments which they called their minds."

Many still believed, as Dr. Edward noted in his highly regarded 1873 tome *Sex and Education*, that "a girl could study and learn, but she could not do all this and retain uninjured health, and a future secure from neuralgia, uterine disease, hysteria, and other derangements of the nervous system." His findings were discounted by the healthful advantages of scholarship and looser clothing for physical education, part of the university routine.

Nothing, it turned out, not even industrious domestic chores, promoted a nourishing flush to the cheek quite like the removal of a girdle and corset, several jumping jacks, and an intellectually stimulating atmosphere.

Despite the abundance of Dr. Edwardses and Henry Adamses in the world, there I was, a college student, living in a dormitory for married couples with Wallace, Wallace rarely home.

The medical field, as we soon discovered, had far more challenging requirements than the domestic sciences, leaving me with plenty of time to ponder, study, read, and discover other interests, and thus grew my enchantment (though Wallace termed it an obsession) with Onata Green.

Three other girls in our department often came to my place for study sessions, but really they were informal gatherings where we smoked, drank, gossiped, argued, discussed, and philosophized.

One of the girls always had a bottle of whiskey (hence the birth of my fondness) and a pack or two of cigarettes. Her father, much to our benefit, was a member of the Seagram's empire, and he indulged his youngest of four with whatever she wanted, including a higher education, a sizable weekly allowance, and an endless supply of Seagram's.

I began to take a relish in the aroma of tobacco and alcohol that greeted Wallace on his returns: dishes stacked in the kitchen, the spectacle of a clump of my dirty underthings mingled with his in a corner of our bedroom.

Thankfully, he was consumed in his studies and didn't complain. "Did you know," he'd say in amazement, stepping over a stack of my books at the floor, "that your brain is eighty percent water?"

Once, his mother came to visit, and she sat at the edge of a faded overstuffed chair, drinking her tea in measured sips from a chipped cup, casting brittle and observant glances around the room.

Her eyes went to a three-inch daddy longlegs working its way across our wall, and she shuddered.

"Get it," she said. "Son: kill it."

Wallace cupped the spider, opened our front door, and set it gently on its way.

I loved him more or as much in that instant than I had when I'd said my marriage vows. I could never have predicted that our relationship would weaken.

At one point, he excused himself to the lavatory, and his mother asked me, "Why do you allow my son to live like this?"

"We're all right," I said.

She didn't say anything, making a sharp and discerning survey of our surroundings, her shoulders pulled back and her face tilted up. I'd dusted before her arrival and set vases of fresh-cut flowers on two tables.

"We're happy," I said.

Her lips pressed in resolve, and she said, "If you cleaned more, it wouldn't be so bad."

I felt a nauseating hatred for her but I swallowed and nodded.

"Are you feeding him well?"

I nodded.

"His stomach has always been sensitive to butter."

I nodded.

"Don't overdo butter."

"No," I said. "Of course not."

"Throw away those awful curtains," she said, flinging a pointed finger their direction. "Buy something decent."

"Sure," I said. I hadn't even noticed the curtains before.

"I'll write a check," she said.

"No," I said.

But the check arrived by post two weeks later, in my name, and without telling Wallace, I cashed the money and took the girls in my department to a feast of a dinner at the best restaurant in town.

We stayed out well beyond a reasonable hour, laughing and eating and drinking, and when I awoke the following morning, I smiled immediately at the remembrance of the cashed check and the resultant revelry.

Not long after, a cousin brought me a large file with letters, documents, tattered notebooks, and a rippled photograph, introducing me to a distant relative.

"You like history," my cousin said. "So you'll like this. I found it at my Grandma's, with a bunch of other stuff."

"Onata Green," I said, looking at her name on the notebook.

No one knew how the items came into her grandmother's possession. Her grandma didn't even remember her own name, much less the packet of memorabilia, suffering, as she did, from dementia.

The university didn't want the file for their historical records, she explained, and it had no financial value. "Believe me, I checked. So," she continued, "because you're sentimental like that, and you love to read and write, here—" and she set them on my table, gifting me.

With my cousin watching, I pulled the photograph from the file, and immediately I tried to hide from my face that I couldn't wait for her to leave.

Across time, Onata Green's sad, intelligent eyes stared at me. She looked comfortable and luxurious sitting in a chair, her black hair stacked in a messy bundle, one hand cupped upward in her lap, the other draped across the armrest. She wore a silky dark dress, revealing her shoulders, the faint outline of a necklace, a formidable body, stocky and secure.

Onata Green died in 1886, the same year I was born, and an envelope contained her death certificate.

She died near the farm where she took her first breath thirty-five years earlier, as the primary sentence in her journal indicated:

I have an affidavit executed by my brother, George Green, seventeen years my senior, stating that I was born on May 21, 1851. He should know as he was sent on horseback to call the doctor to preside over the event. No governmental entity has ever, to my knowledge, taken note of my birth, though there is documentation of my mother's death, and a certificate, for in giving me life, she lost hers; that is the reason for the affidavit.

I survived, she did not. I have often wondered what course my life would have taken had I known a mother and father.

Onata's father died from typhoid six months before her birth, and three of her siblings before him in quick succession went to their graves, leaving George, who also happened to be my father's uncle's cousin's son, though I never met him.

The impulse to write came from Onata's need to unleash feelings and experiences, and also, she wrote: "Inasmuch as I have always had difficulty recounting, I have decided to reduce my thoughts to prose so that I may be able to finish, without being reminded by George's showing of fingers, that I have told that one before."

Perhaps, she mused, a wanderer might come across her words "to find and know me long after my skin and bones dissolve."

The urge, she admitted, was a habit connected to her troubled soul. "Nowhere else can I unfold my inner life with freedom."

After graduation, after Wallace established his practice as a doctor, and after we moved to our home, I returned to Onata Green.

I decided to write her biography.

I visited the farm where Onata was raised, looked at photographs, collected information and facts, until I felt that I knew Onata Green and her beloved brother George.

I didn't finish, though I have a detailed working outline.

My incomplete Onata biography became indistinguishable from my stunted athletic career, and eventually I gave up on running, on babies, on myself, and on Onata.

I got this far:

Start at the beginning, at the farm, which, Onata had been told, had been purchased by her grandfather, who took title from the government, and who later lost his life after a drunken brawl, clobbered on the back of his head with a shovel by the same sober foe when he was turned and unaware, drinking from a water spring.

Her grandfather married her grandmother to help with his primary concern: building a log house and settling. Wood was plentiful, and a stream—too small to have a name—ran through the home place.

Her grandparents were religious and her brother George once said that Revelations was her grandmother's favorite book of the Bible. Onata wondered why, for she found it lacking, except in its vivid images.

Onata didn't know her maternal grandparents, but George told her stories. She was named after her maternal grandmother. The grandparents used to make regular calls when her parents had been alive.

The grandfather always had an apple in his pocket, but took his time about giving it to George. He wore leather pants when he was young, and he liked to proclaim that this was how he attracted Grandma Onata.

On cold mornings, he would drag the pants into bed to warm them before putting them on. He courted his future wife, though she lived eight miles away, which was really getting around in those days.

He was especially impressed that Grandma Onata could play a guitar and a mouth organ at the same time, the mouth organ held by a frame around her neck. She was part Mohawk and sometimes wore a stovepipe hat.

A remarkable woman, with ideas way ahead of her time, Grandma Onata took George to a lecture about sex matters, given by a woman. It was a very embarrassing experience, and he didn't like discussing it.

Grandma Onata held the shocking notion that women's legs should not be hid any more than a man's. She insisted on piloting the horse buggy, and she taught George table manners that stood him in good stead.

Once, when George was four, Grandma Onata was seated in the buggy talking to George and Onata's mother, who was standing alongside. George asked, "Where's your whip?" and Grandma Onata raised her right hand holding the whip high. The whip had been out of sight on the other side of the horse.

George always liked her for that silent reply. In her honor, he tried to interact with children as equals, and without an adult's standard patronizing manner.

As Grandma Onata got older, and after her husband died, she became more peculiar. She wore her husband's pants underneath her dresses, and she walked circles around the house, walked and walked, so that she wore a path in the dirt. She continued to drive the buggy, sometimes veering close to the trees.

Once, a squirrel ran across the road ahead of them, and Grandmother Onata handed George the lines, jumped from the buggy, then over the fence and into the woods, picking up a stick as she ran toward the tree where the squirrel was headed.

When she reached the tree, she hit around blindly and killed the squirrel. She brought it back to the buggy and made George hold it by its tail because, she said, it might come alive.

So he did, all the way home, and then he buried it.

Shortly before Grandma Onata died, she told George what had happened to her as a young girl of thirteen, years before she met her husband.

One morning, George built a fire in the fireplace and asked Onata to sit so that he could speak with her. When he told Onata, she could tell that it was important and that he'd been struggling with how to let her know.

He said that what Grandma Onata had told him was a vulgar story, and that it troubled him to speak it aloud. But he also believed it would help Onata through her life, knowing that her grandmother was fierce and that Onata carried her not only in name, but also in blood.

George was right: it was this story that shaped and strengthened Onata.

George was thirteen when Grandma Onata told him what had happened to her at the same age, and because he was so young, and because the story shocked him, he could not remember the circumstances that had led Grandma Onata to be captured by a soldier and help captive deep in the woods.

The man had had his way with Onata and was resting near the campfire, naked, except for his revolver hanging from its holster at his hip. He'd held a knife to Onata's throat and sang in her ear while he violated her, just cutting at her skin so that her blood dripped down her front. She was tall for her age, almost as tall as the soldier, and brown as a tree. He drank from a bottle and ate grilled rabbit meat, and he told her, between bites, that when he was done with her, he would kill her.

Onata sat naked with her knees pulled to her chin, blood dribbling. The fire popped and the soldier reached for a stick, shuffling the wood in its pit, mesmerized by the dancing flames, crouched with his back to Onata.

In a stealth quiet duck walk, she moved to him. When he bent forward, she reached and seized the dark mass hanging between his legs, twisting in a vise-like grip. A noise issued from him like an animal, and he hurled forward, missing the fire, curled into a ball. She ran and ran and ran and ran and heard the distant report of bullets and never saw him again.

The image of her grandmother reaching and grabbing the naked soldier's genitals came to Onata with frequency, at times both trying and easy, and whether she beckoned it forth or not.

When Onata was seven, George courted and married a woman named Lulu, and they raised Onata as their own, and had four children besides. Onata was prone to reminding them that they weren't her real father and mother. Lulu's father was a wealthy bank owner, and George worked for him but continued to farm.

One of Onata's earliest memories of Lulu was when Lulu took her to the city to buy her better dresses. Onata became sick on the train and vomited in the aisle, and a porter had to clean the mess.

She also remembered George taking her to town. One time, Lulu told him to bring home eggs. He was a great jokester. He bought hickory nuts and sent Onata home with them, telling her to say to Lulu, "Here are your eggs."

Either because she was so truthful, or because she was afraid to lie when the proof was so immediate and convincing, or because she didn't want to participate in a farce, Onata said, "Here are your eggs but they are hickory nuts."

Onata frequently got into trouble. She cut the other kids' hair; she put Lulu's knitting needles in the sofa, and George sat on them; she baptized the kids in a bathtub, saying, "I baptize thee in the name of Onata, the son, and the Holy Ghost."

During Onata's fourteenth year, Lulu died of consumption, and George remarried Lulu's younger sister, Ida. The sisters had made the arrangement before Lulu's death. Onata didn't approve of the quick change, and Lulu's passing brought forth the devastation and deprivation Onata felt at not having known a birth mother or father.

At fourteen, she grieved! Often she went into a corn patch in the orchard and cried. Once, George found her with her face buried in a dishtowel, sobbing, and they both grew alarmed because she couldn't stop.

When his kind words and sympathy didn't help, George reminded her that he, too, had lost his parents and siblings, and that she did not have a dominion on grief, and she finally was able to dry her eyes.

By her fifteenth year, she shifted into a deep rebellion and took to protesting ideas of proper behavior. She disappeared often, most notably from church on Sundays. Clever in mind and body, quick to learn and graceful, she joined a boys' lacrosse team, until she was discovered and banished.

George had trouble keeping her at school. She was a wandering girl, and they never quite knew where she was. In frustration,

George sent her to a Quaker boarding school for girls, ten miles from the farm.

At this time, there was an explosion in her heart.

Life made no sense, and she understood that sanity was as feeble as life itself. Death came to everyone and seemed a reprieve. She began to fantasize. She would look at the mountains and think, *The mountains will be here tomorrow and I will not.* Yet fear kept her from suicide, and even more, the thought of Grandma Onata, her namesake. She was connected, and it was Grandma Onata's blood that kept her alive.

She became sick with pneumonia and was sent back to the farm in a very dangerous condition. George cared for her, spooning medicine and soup in her mouth and giving her clandestine sips of whiskey. Ida went to town and brought back ice, feeding her ice chips. These kind deeds almost undid her.

Her convalescence began, and each day, she gained strength and stamina. One morning she woke to the sun breaking through the curtains, filling the room with a greenish gold, and her heart luxuriated in the sweetness of its survival. She wanted to live again! She went to the window and watched the beams swaying through the thick foliage of the sugar maples.

Onata learned how to give herself to the currents of life, without demanding anything, and without thinking about tomorrow, or the day before.

It was not long after her seventeenth birthday that she met Edward Nedlan at a dinner party, and terror blazed through her like a fire, just from his look. It was mutual. They sat across from each other at the table, throwing stares. She was fully grown, and although not beautiful, she found that her dresses suddenly needed more room up top. Her corsets had tightened and were bursting from the heft. Men looked and their eyes stayed, and she knew that she gained a power hitherto not in her possession. They weren't looking at her face but at what was directly below.

Though married, Edward was alone that night, his wife home with the flu, and he passed Onata a note, asking her to meet him the following afternoon at a park. She didn't consider not showing. She saw him standing near a rose garden, and when she went to him, she felt as if a coal were burning inside her, its ashes having been blown from it.

The Onata women were tall and substantial. He was a full head shorter and of lesser weight. He remarked on the difference, saying that she might want to pat his head like a child, even though he was her elder by seven years. But she could tell that it attracted him.

They sat at a bench and talked. His voice was soft and husky, and it burrowed inside her, so that even as he spoke of tame topics, she felt as if he had his hand inside her corset, at her skin, and was rubbing there.

He wore his hat turned down at the front, shading his face, a line of shadow halted at his lips. "I can't see your eyes," she commented. He removed his hat. Oh! What a man! What a face! Wide-open, ravenous. She watched his lips and nostrils bringing in air, and she wanted him to breathe her through him and take possession.

His head was large in comparison to his body, with lips soft in a continual pout, more accustomed to melancholy than joy. His chin square and strong, and his skin brown from sun, a red-brown at the back of his neck, from bending forward mid-row, sun striking. His hair was black with a purple-oil sheen, and he fingered it, pulling it from his forehead, although it retained a bump from his hat-line.

She could tell that his muscles were tight and compact, his thighs most pronounced, flexed against his pant legs. His shirt was of a thin white material, so that his dark chest hairs barely showed beneath, like the blurred lines beneath the ice in an ice rink. His smell reminded her of her childhood dog. She loved to bury her face in the dog's fur, for it comforted her with its dirt and animal odor.

His face wasn't classically handsome, but his complicated character came through, attracting her. She decided that men reveal beauty through character in their physical appearance, whereas women's beauty and attractiveness depend on surface physical traits. What is beneath does not count for women as it does for men.

When he took the hat off, the sun shone on his face, revealing his eyes, and that was when she was permanently undone. Deep brown and marked with a golden shifting of emotions, big and open and sensitive, and ringed by eyelashes more typical on a girl.

When he put his eyes fully to hers, she blushed and her mouth went dry. She swallowed three times, summoned Grandma Onata, and found her tongue. "I fear you," she said.

After a long and strained pause, with all her willpower, she informed him that she was due at home.

"Of course," he said. "I've taken enough of your time."

The next few months passed without incident, and she gathered information about Edward, careful not to attract suspicion. Born to Irish parents, he married his childhood sweetheart at sixteen. Their home on Toronto Island had been swept by a storm, washing ashore several miles from his father's hotel where he worked. He began sculling the difference from work and home, several kilometers each day, developing his skill, which led him to register in his first regatta. He finished third to last, and the newspaper claimed that he didn't possess the drive of a competitor, but had the deportment of a daydreamer.

The following month at another dinner party, Onata happened upon Edward and his wife, Mary, outside near the garden.

Edward introduced the women and then excused himself to get a drink, leaving Mary and Onata alone. Small and pretty, with fair hair and dark eyes, Mary commented on the evening, and they agreed that it was pleasant.

More small talk, and then Mary excused herself, perhaps noticing a remote coldness that kept Onata from thinking of Mary as a person—a flesh-and-blood woman.

Onata would look back on their strange exchange as a moral failure on her part, the first of many.

As soon as Mary left, Edward came from behind a tree, as if he'd been hiding and waiting. He looked pale and sick, and when she asked him if he needed to sit or if she should get him a glass of water, he said harshly, "It's not water that I need!"

He took her elbow and guided her further from the party, to the edge near a gate. The lights from the house shimmered, and laughter and music carried. A full moon made the night visible, and near a tree was another couple in an embrace.

He led her to the gate's opening, and soon they were hidden in the woods. He breathed heavily beside her, and all at once he said, "What is this? What are you doing to me?"

She worried that she'd offended him without knowing how or why, and she stood in confusion, her breathing irregular, and her heart racing within her bosom.

He took her elbows, encouraged her to a kneel. Then he was kneeling and his head was in her hair, filling his nostrils with her. She was incredulous, and soon they were in a violent passion, his face pressed against her breast.

He paused, took a breath, unbuttoned his shirt, and guided her hand across him, so that she felt his muscular form. He looked as if he would cry, and he said, "I'm a sinner!" and her heart flooded with tenderness. "Who are you?" he asked, so close she tasted his breath, salty and sour and, "What's happening?"

"I've no idea," she said.

"Don't stop," he urged, guiding her hand, "don't stop, don't stop, please."

In the midst of their passion, Onata had an intimation that she would come to need him terribly, and that this would lead to a terrible outcome.

So began Edward's subsequent winning streak, connected to Onata, sprung from carnal greed. The following morning, he competed and crossed the finish bow by bow with his rival's boat, but he raised his fist in clear celebration of his victory, so that ultimately the judges agreed.

Onata wore a face of innocence and became practiced at deception. Alert and inventive, they carried on their liaisons undetected, meeting in a shack at the pier where Edward kept his boat. He created a bed out of blankets, and there was an iron woodstove to keep them warm.

An old widower who lived close by saw them, but he didn't care about Onata and gave a winking approval to Edward.

After they exhausted their bodies in vice, they talked strategy. Onata helped Edward develop his rowing technique: thrusting his legs and balancing on his sliding seat, so that his height and weight wouldn't hamper him against larger opponents. He got his stroke perfected not by the angle of his oars but by his body angle and stride, the power coming from his legs.

When he competed, she did all the worrying for him.

She had him squat and jump, squat and jump, squat and jump, building his thighs even larger, and she counted and encouraged. They did arm and leg exercises and calisthenics.

She loved to lie with their bodies' sweat mingling and their muscles tight, delirious in their physical strain and pleasures.

Once, Mary had Onata to lunch, and Onata taught the two youngest children hopscotch. She went not from curiosity, but to stifle suspicion. She was large and not beautiful, so that once Mary got a good look at her, she felt that Mary would never suspect. Lemon cake was served, the same color as Mary's hair. It seemed that Onata chewed pieces of rubber.

Mary smiled and smiled, her face ordinary and jolly, and Onata's soul shrank. Their conversation was awkward and brief, and Onata was not asked back again.

When Mary and the children went to visit Mary's parents for two weeks, Onata and Edward rejoiced, unabashedly taking over the house as their personal quarters for pleasure. Nary a space went untainted, in full daylight, no less, on floor and on table, in corners and closets. It didn't matter, they were helpless, and this included the wedding bed and the children's beds.

They rationalized their eagerness, convinced that by fully engaging their desires, they would extinguish them and finally leave their impropriety behind. But their appetites grew larger, beyond anything they could have controlled or predicted.

There was no denying that their lovemaking, along with Onata's coaching, improved Edward's confidence, to the point that he became convinced that he was undefeatable.

He traveled to compete, leaving his family and Onata to pine, and he became known as a ruthless competitor, humiliating his challengers.

Before races, as his opponents watched, he blew kisses to their wives, girlfriends, and mothers.

After crossing the finish lines, he rowed back to his rivals, and crossed again, beating them twice. He pretended to sleep, head bowed, and when his opponents approached, he awoke with a dramatic flair and won easily. He rowed zigzags, his rivals struggling in mortification in their straight lines.

At times, Onata wondered if she'd created a monster. He would do anything to win, and then delight in his adversaries' defeat.

You don't really know a person, Onata concluded, until you see how that person responds to winning.

One afternoon, George confronted Onata. "You're a mistress to a scoundrel!"

She denied it.

"You're my sister!" he said. "You think I wouldn't know?"

He threatened to obliterate Edward's manhood with a well-aimed rifle shot.

"You don't love him," he said, and she said, "How would you know?'"

She was frustrated that she couldn't quit Edward, and she suffered bouts of guilt.

Yet there was only a moment of regret as they engaged in the physical act, a vast sadness, and then all would become a tidal wave of euphoria that rendered her an amnesiac, temporarily sweeping aside all practicality, conscience, and negative thoughts.

Edward left to compete in England and while he was gone, one night, Mary came to the farm after supper.

From the window, George noticed her approaching, and he sent Onata to the door, telling her in a reprimanding whisper, "Keep it outdoors, as far away as possible. There are children here."

Onata's terror was met with more terror when she saw Mary at the doorway. "Hello," Onata said, attempting casualness, but her face strained and her voice sounded hollow. It seemed in bad manners not to smile, so she forced one.

Mary was quiet and stared at her. Remembering George's request, Onata suggested they leave, and Mary followed her down the pathway.

They walked for a long time in silence, and then, under a full moon, Mary stopped. "This," she said, screwing her lips and twisting her wedding band from her finger, "my dear prostitute, belongs to you."

Onata wanted to deny but her face wouldn't obey. Everything in her life was obliterated in a heavy shame, as if a giant hand came down from the sky and clubbed her.

Onata wouldn't take the ring, and Mary kept thrusting it at her, pushing at her chest. "I loved you," she said, "trusted you," perhaps confusing Onata with Edward, and the whole time she kept weeping and shoving and thrusting.

Then she made a giant swing, flinging the ring into the grass, and with her other hand, striking Onata across the mouth so that she tasted blood.

"No, no, no!" Mary cried, and she ran in the direction that she threw, landing at her knees in a frantic search.

Onata went to a crawl beside her, hunting in the dark, swallowing her blood. "Sorry, sorry," she said.

Mary told Onata to shut her mouth, and she did.

Onata wept silently for it seemed unfair to cry with Mary.

They searched, and then Mary rose, her dress and face muddied. She stared down at Onata. Onata couldn't bear her eyes and turned her face.

After Mary left, Onata looked until George made her come inside. She looked the next day, and the next, and she found the ring and sent it to Mary by post.

Edward returned from his victory in England to his failure at home. Months passed, and Onata and Edward stayed away from each other. Onata helped Ida tend to the children, and she worked in the garden and cooked and cleaned. She took up sewing and knitting and other hobbies that she had previously scorned. Her stubborn and rebellious nature had transformed to compliant, submissive, and helpful. Internally full of turmoil, she wore a placid appearance and tried to be of use.

Edward suffered one defeat after another, losing to weaker opponents. During one race, he had a near-collision with a chartered steamer. After another defeat, he claimed that a foul had been perpetrated against him and filed a complaint, only for the referee to side against him, terming him a poor loser.

Late one afternoon, in a state of high agitation, Edward came to Onata. She wouldn't let him inside, and he stood at the doorway.

The sun was low and the wind had picked up. He took a handkerchief from his pocket, pressed it against his reddened nostrils. "I need you," he said.

She told him, "You need me to win," and he looked down.

He admitted that their passion and his victories were connected. Without her, he said, winning was impossible, like trying to exhale and inhale at the same time.

Onata was exhausted, angry, guilty, and in pain. She barely slept. "You," she said, "are a horrible man. I wish I'd never met you," and that finally got Edward to leave.

Thus began the second explosion in her soul. There was no denying that she had sinned against Mary and her children. She couldn't justify her behavior, and she couldn't bear to live with what she'd done.

But it was not only sin, for in truth she'd lived with sin before. It was not only the betrayal. It was that she'd been winning alongside Edward, tasting his victories.

Onata wasn't allowed to participate in athletics, but she'd found her way to competition through Edward. She, like Edward, would do anything to win.

She was unnerved by how giddy his victories made her feel. It shouldn't matter that much. It shouldn't feel that good. Waves of emotion washed over her each time. Relief and elation and a hysterical serenity, because she believed that she'd earned those victories through him.

She was supposed to be a different person, a better person, not a person who believed winning was everything. What kind of woman was she?

When they declared Edward the victor, internally she took her position beside him, a champion. She lived for success.

Their sin and perfidy had wrought a beast that fed on victory. Discovered and shamed, they lost, and losing was awful compared with winning, and endured.

Losing, it turned out, was imperative, and she needed to fit it inside her and live with its constancy.

Onata trained with a midwife, became an assistant. For the next eight years, she traveled and aided in the delivery of babies. She also became an advocate of contraception, delivering pamphlets that outlined various birth control techniques.

A pamphlet was included in the file, containing radical opinions, penned by Onata:

1. Women are not procreative serfs.
2. Motherhood does not make a woman happy.
3. Sexual intercourse need not be solely for procreation.

When the midwife passed away, Onata took on her duties, having been cultivated for this purpose. She found an assistant, began training her as she'd been trained. She read the Bible, prayed, devoted herself to others.

Civic-minded and well liked, she nevertheless kept to herself. Men attempted to court her, but she was unresponsive to flattery and attention, having decided that she'd abused and worn out that portion of her life long before.

Mary did not utilize Onata's midwifery services for the birth of her baby, and another, and a third and final, making seven children total, instead relying on family members. But with each birth, she took her scissors to the local newspaper's announcements, and posted and mailed the clippings to Onata, with her initials scribbled over the type to ensure the recipient of their sender.

Edward's regatta days ended after a trail of bitter losses, and he tended bar at his father's hotel. He retained his popularity. The crowds had loved his crazy antics, though his opponents had not. The bar was covered with photographs of his earlier victories, ever reminding him that he'd once been a champion.

No matter how old he became, no matter what he did with his life, whether he lived or died, whether he was happily married or divorced, whether he was a good father or not, the photos acted as a shrine.

Yet he became known for an adage: "No matter how much you win," he would tell his customers, "if you don't win the last one, you're a loser."

Edward sent Onata a letter on fine onionskin paper, undated. She saved it in the file, and folded Mary's birth announcements within, as a statement and reminder.

My dearest Onata,

I cannot hope that you would begin to understand my forwardness and bad manners in writing to you, after your specific demand that I disappear from your life. I would rather die having tried than having not. I must tell you my feelings and the only way to do so is abruptly and without too much thought.

I pray to Our Lord and Savior that you forgive my impropriety and read with an open heart, for HE forgives me and knows all, and loves me for the sake of what I have to say.

My heart and soul are yours. I lost them to you the instant you looked at me across the table at the dinner party long ago. That was my fate! I did not request it! You talk of winning and losing. I lost everything to you. You have stolen me.

I see your face and hear your voice. I watch you every night in my sleep. We belong together and always have and you know it in your heart! Our bodies belong as one.

If it were not for my own cowardice, I would come take you right now. Your brother be damned! I would tell you these things in person! I ache for you. I only know sorrow.

This is a matter of life or death. For you see you have taken my heart with you, and there is nothing left for me. I am pretending through life. I am a shadow. I continue to breathe though I am only a ghost.

Please take me back into your arms. I want to live there. I remain forever lost, and sustain myself only through memories.

You believe that my love for you is based on victories. But that was a benefit and a sign of the power. It was not the love itself but the outcome. It was our shared victory, shared fears, shared trust, and shared bodies.

You torture me by brutally exposing me to your love and trust, and then stealing it from me, as if you cared nothing for me at all.

I would leave Mary and the children if you asked. I would do anything for you.

Please don't ask me to live without you. I cannot feel life without you.

Without you, all is dead.

Have compassion.

> *Yours eternally,*
> E. N.

In the spring of 1886, Onata was in a crowded Metropolitan Street Railway, on her way home from a visit with a patient. She looked out the window and wondered what she would do if she saw Edward. She decided that he would be lost by the time she could make her way through the car with her medical bag.

Upon her arrival, she walked across the street to a beauty shop, deciding to treat herself. She was in the chair, and she watched the hands of the clock on the wall inch along. Three thirty-three, three thirty-four, three thirty-five. An icy coldness went through her for no discernible reason. Her pulse quickened, and she asked for a glass of water. She felt as though thousands of ants were crawling on her and through her, inside her mouth, everywhere.

She drank the water, but the sensation wouldn't leave. She paid and left, her hair half-finished. That was Saturday afternoon.

Monday morning she received word that Edward had been killed while working at the bar.

A local disgruntled drunk reached inside his jacket and drew out a pistol, aimed it at Edward's chest. According to witnesses,

Edward said, "Do it, do it, do it," and the drunk finally complied, pulling the trigger. An ongoing argument, a witness said, existed between the men, concerning Edward's cutoff limit.

But at that same trial, Edward's life insurance company proposed a scheme on Edward's part: he paid the drunk to shoot, rained the drunk in alcohol to steel his nerves. But still at that critical point, the drunk faltered, and thus Edward's reminder: *do it, do it, do it.*

The jury decided otherwise, and the drunk was sentenced to life imprisonment. Edward's wife and children collected on the life insurance policy after all, as it was considered not a suicide but a murder.

The time of the shooting was when Onata was in the chair looking at the clock.

Soon after, Onata had a second bout of pneumonia. George and Ida cared for her, but she became worse and was hospitalized.

She lay in the hospital for a week and two days. Before her hospitalization, she predicted her death, telling George, "It is done. I go where Spirit takes me."

I began to write and ponder the life of Onata Green, but the day came when I sat at my desk to ponder and write and I couldn't continue, for I would never know what happened as it happened, or what it meant.

Onata's story would be filtered and dirtied through me.

Now I understand that Onata made me think that I could be a serious intellect and an athlete.

But I couldn't finish, and I confused her story with mine.

Instead of burning my notes and work, I burned my running shoes in our yard, and Wallace came home to a scorched pit and called the doctor for my head. But I saved her file and my outline with my journals, in the closet and then in the safe deposit box at the bank.

Often I've thought of Onata thinking, *The mountains will be here tomorrow and I will not,* but then seeing her great grandmother's hand reaching and gripping the soldier's genitals, twisting, insisting, demanding, and saving her life, and that was enough for Onata, and I've discovered through the years that the same holds for me.

Chapter Seven

Winning and Losing

―――

I

It was after the 100-metres, Bonnie's race, that Jack got the idea for promoting and expanding his Athletic Club, taking advantage of the press's fascination with the Peerless Four, and using the Dream Girl's image, their ideal specimen (his too), as a promotional tool. He wanted to change the course of women's athletics and to save our girls from the repercussions of winning and losing. But I'm getting ahead of myself.

The *Albertic* steamed up the St. Lawrence River, and once we moved into the open ocean, our wake frothing behind us in two creamy trails that merged into one, the girls had become accustomed to drinking milk for seasickness since "it doesn't hurt going down or coming up," as Farmer put it.

Discipline and routine ruled our lives, a rigid schedule for the eight-day trip: a morning saltwater bath at eight, breakfast at nine, a workout at ten-thirty, practice until noon, lunch at one, a walk from two-thirty to three-thirty, deck games, dinner at six, dancing in the evening, bed at ten, and a final checkup from me at ten thirty. The entire ship was transformed into a large gymnasium, and it was something to behold: promenade decks covered with cork to make a track, a boxing ring and fencing strip, a place for calisthenics. The pistol team had target equipment set up. There was a small canvas pool where the swimmers swam suspended from a rope anchored above. The javelin throwers used javelins with ropes attached and threw them out to sea, dragging them back.

Bonnie and Flo had to be watched the most, with Ginger and Danny following close behind. Flo sneaked out one night with a male high jumper, but I found them before anything happened.

There was one night when I heard a noise coming from the dining room, but the girls were just having a contest to see who could touch this hanging light. They'd moved the tables, and the noise was the sound of them dragging the tables to give room. So we all put some money in a pot to see if anyone could touch it. Everyone tried. Even me, and five or six of the boys from the track team. No one could touch it, and then Farmer took this crazy, wild leaping run. She jumped and her fingertips skirted the bottom so that it swung slightly.

One of the men's track coaches, J. R. Cornelius, would have nothing to do with our team, coaching or otherwise. "This is dangerous," he said, adding that the spectacle of our lightly-clad, sweating team engaged in strenuous activities had an unsettling moral effect on his men. "He doesn't like women," Jack said. "He really doesn't like women."

There was considerable table discussion among the male coaches and officials about whether our girls' athletic activities would affect their health later on. It was a favored topic. Some argued that they would have heart trouble, and there were doubts about whether they'd have children. There was so much discussion about the pros and cons of women in competition that I got tired of it all.

My job had become strangely culinary, and in Amsterdam, our first meal at the pension consisted of an orange with dry pith inside, no juice to spoon out, and a hard roll, with a small and useless curl of butter. A husky woman with a black mustache was in charge, and I fostered a relationship with her, so that she would make oatmeal in the mornings, and for lunches and dinners, either a round of steak, roast beef, chicken, lamb chops, and peas and spinach, and, occasionally, fried potatoes, though the girls regularly got gas from this treat.

Amsterdam was wet and sometimes cold but a different type of wet and cold than we were used to. Instead of outright raining, the moisture hung in the air, as if we mostly lived inside a cloud for six weeks, and the cold crept inside you before you even knew you were cold, refusing to leave entirely once you figured it out, even after a hot bath.

That north wind blowing off Norway and Sweden, down into Amsterdam, was all kinds of cold.

I did my best to ignore the newspapers, following my own ban that I imposed on the girls, but whatever was printed made them crowd favorites, and at the opening ceremony, they heard their names being shouted when we marched, along with Canada! Canada! Canada! We wore scarlet hats and heels, white blazers piped with red, white stockings, pleated white skirts, and silk blouses, and each of their faces lighted to the sound of her name, setting her apart, except for Ginger, who seemed to go deeper inside herself.

There was also the big cheer that went "Rah, rah, USA, A-M-E-R-I-C-A," and the Americans didn't dip their flag when they marched past the receiving stand, all going back to the 1908 London Games. One of the New York Irish Whales refused to dip the flag to the English king as a demonstration against British rule in Ireland, and now they don't dip, just because they're America.

The French cheer went, "Un, deux, trois; un, deux, trois; un, deux, trois, quatre, cinq," with the crowd clapping their hands together.

The grand stadium was a swamp that had been drilled with holes and filled with a million cubic yards of sand. A Dutch detective took my camera to protect the photographic monopoly the government had sold to one firm. But I got it back, along with an apology, by flashing my official badge.

Queen Wilhelmina decided not to show for the opening ceremony to avoid any religious controversy, since it was a Sunday, but over forty thousand others had no religious objections, and a large number more were unable to get tickets, jamming the streets and blocking the stadium, forcing the Finnish team to scramble over the wall to gain entrance.

Speeches were made, bands played, and when I looked back, Farmer and Ginger had removed their shoes. They hurt, Farmer mouthed, and I didn't respond, for even the thought of Farmer in heels was wrong. We applauded the hoisting of the Olympic flag, and then it was up and flapping, its five-colored interlocking circles representing the five major land masses of the world, and at least one of the colors of the circles appearing in every national flag in the world. There was the oath, and the contestants agreed to compete in "the true spirit of sportsmanship for the glory of sport and the honor of country." Then a blast of trumpets and the roar of a cannon, and forty-six pigeons blooming skyward, each with a ribbon bearing the color of one of the competing nations tied to its neck, and Farmer said, "Better duck, unless you want to be crowned with something other than laurels," and we laughed.

So the games began with much pomp, and we ate our meals and slept and ignored the papers, and I soothed the girls. It took a while to adjust to Amsterdam. Bonnie said that everything looked old, and Flo said that that was because everything was old, and Farmer said that the air even *tasted* old.

We kept busy with practice to take our minds off home. The girls had never had an adventure like this before and would never have one like it after, and we all knew it and tried to appreciate without being homesick. Then Hugh Williams, a shy, small, unassuming nineteen-year-old high school student from Vancouver who'd taken a shine to Ginger and vice versa, won the gold medal in the 100-metres. He had this awkward elegance to his running style, sprinting straight up, with high knees, and at the finish line he leapt at the tape with his arms extended wildly. The crowd sounded like an ocean, with Hugh standing on the podium not saying a word and moving only to bow his head to receive his gold medal, his hair falling over his forehead.

Hugh's coach was a dictator, not letting Hugh leave his room, rubbing him with coconut oil, making him practice his starts by leaping forward and crashing into a mattress propped against the wall, so that all the way at the women's side of the pension, we could hear the soft *boom* from his body smacking against it. But now that Hugh had won, everyone was calling the coach a genius, wanting to shake his hand.

Of the six finalists remaining from a field of thirty-one for the women's 100-metre heats, one was Bonnie, favored to win as the world-record holder. In the dread of the slow minutes before the final race, Bonnie gave me a brief, dazed glance, and my heart tried to leap from my chest. I was at the side, closer than the spectators in the stands but not with the athletes. The air was spongy and full of drizzle.

The runners paced back and forth, jiggling and jumping, and Bonnie was avoiding my eyes now, shaking out her legs whether they needed shaking or not, and I was thinking, *Oh hell*, pacing up and back, because I couldn't sit. Each of the runners jumped up and down, shook out her legs and arms, and did other private, concentrated, ritualized calisthenics, both exorcist-like and prayerful, hoping to bring divine grace into her body, while at the same time casting out fears, worries, strains.

I was remembering Bonnie's saying she had to win, and how that didn't bode well when you needed something and wanted it too much, because that was the kind of world we lived in. You couldn't get exactly what you wanted, no matter how much you tried, and she shouldn't have wanted it so badly, but it was too late. There she was lined up for the race.

I'm not one of the anointed athletes. Yet we're connected, and as a spectator, I'm necessary to witness, transcribe, and bring to life the experience. Besides, if you ask a great athlete to describe the secret behind her athletic genius, she most likely won't respond adequately. "I gave it a hundred percent," she might say, or, "God was on my side!" or "I was just able to take it to the next level," or another variant of the athletes' interchangeable clichés. We want more. We want to know what it means. Why her, and not us? But she can't explain the blind nothingness at the essence of her athletic gift. She's required to burrow into this nothingness, with an ascetic concentration, in order to win. She has to give everything over, not hold back, truly clean and free and full of maximum effort, and therefore reduced in complexity. For her athletic genius to have meaning, for us to understand, we need to be spectators.

I watched a male javelin thrower slogging in his sideways motion, hurling his spear. The male broad jumpers bounded around, and the high jumpers were taking their run-ups. Then my attention was back on Bonnie, as she dug her feet in for the start, her shoulders dipping down. The front of her white jersey bore a red maple leaf that looked like a large bloody handprint. She and Farmer had cut the sleeves to allow freer movement, and her jersey billowed over her shorts like a sail in the breeze.

She'd been sick that morning, cramping from her period. In the white-hot event of the 100-metres, everything had to be perfect, and I saw that her back leg was shaking. For a second I was inside her body—one big jolting nerve.

So when she broke before the gun, taking the German girl with her, I wasn't surprised even though I wanted to be. Both were charged with a false start and warned by the starter that a second false start would mean disqualification.

The six lined up again, and the German command "Auf die Plätze," and then "Fertig" came as the order for the set position, and Bonnie was down, dug in, and—oh hell—she sprang and broke to a roar from the stands. My heart jumped so hard that

I thought my head would burst off, and then Bonnie's face was on mine, a ghost look—a giant blank nothing look that swallowed me whole—and the starter walked down her lane and waved her off the track.

Bonnie stood unbelieving for a moment, shaking her head. Her face went red and she started blinking. The crowd was making noises—booing, clapping—they couldn't decide what they felt. Then a spasm passed through Bonnie's body and her face contorted and the tears came.

I approached and led her to the side and watched as a third attempt was made to get the runners underway, but then the German had a second false start. She responded the opposite of Bonnie, by shaking her fist under the starter's nose and threatening her, and she had to be dragged from the scene by two officials.

I had Bonnie sitting near the starting line and I was hovering over her, trying to quiet her, but she was grieving loud. I pulled her to a pile of cushions on the grass, where we remained, her head buried in her arms and her body shaking with sobs.

I saw Jack, his mouth open, and the reporters taking their notes, writing down all the reasons girls shouldn't be here—they were too emotional and fragile and couldn't handle competition and were prone to attacks of hysteria—and there was Bonnie, giving herself over to tears, proving them right. We were competing on a trial basis, and our future participation depended on us, and when I tried to remind her, she wouldn't listen, because she had messed everything up already and couldn't hear.

Farmer came and relieved me, taking Bonnie by the elbow and leading her back to the pension and to her room, where she continued to cry, making up for not crying when her mother had been hit by a car and she heard the screeches and screams and imagined it from the inside. Crying for the man she loved, Coach Frank, who loved her and was married with a child due. She cried and cried, and we thought she might not stop, and her face and eyes puffed and went red but she kept on crying. She cried for all sorts of reasons, but mostly she cried because she never got to run, and she was favored to win gold. Training and dreaming of winning, telling herself in the mirror 125 times every night, Hello Bonnie Brody, gold-medal winner, and she never got to run and that made no kind of sense and she cried because that was the world she lived in.

That night, I could barely keep my eyes open, wanting to fall into a dream with no competitions, no winning or losing, no disappointments. On my way to my room, hungering for nothing but my pillow, the clerk saw me and gave me a note. I read the note and heard Jack's voice saying, "Jesus Christ, Mel, get over here now," and he didn't have to tell me where to go.

I headed to Bonnie's room, but not before getting a pack of cigarettes and lighting one, to hell with who might see me, standing there for a moment in the lobby, sucking it down in a hurry, sedating my nerves.

Jack was sitting outside Bonnie's room, as if he'd propped himself on the wall and slid down in defeat. When he saw me, he stood and walked to me, grabbed my arm and kissed me on the mouth before I could object, which I did once his lips left my face.

"Sorry," he said, and I objected again, saying that I might just quit, and for a second I imagined it, a powerful feeling, but then it was gone.

Jack slid back to his sitting position and I sat beside him, and we passed his flask some, and he told me that he needed me, and I knew that it was true and said as much.

He twitched his head the direction of the door and said, "I'm worried. She might do something stupid. It's quiet in there; maybe she's sleeping, but I doubt it. I don't think she's got a bottle. She won't let me in, won't let anyone in," and I said that I'd try.

"I got a key," he said, fishing in his pocket and handing it to me. "Got it from the front desk. Said it was an emergency, and I suppose it is."

"Where's Flo?" I asked, since Bonnie and Flo were rooming together.

"With the sisters, sleeping on the floor."

I shook my head, thinking of them crammed in the room, Flo on the floor. Bonnie's selfishness angered me, no matter how much she was suffering.

"The newspapers," I said, "are going to bury us."

"They already have. They're having a field day."

"Trial basis," I said.

"The girls don't understand," he said. He paused, gave me a probing look, and then I could tell that he was about to say something to try to lighten my mood.

"You must love me," he said, "because you're not working for money, and you're not working for fun."

"No," I said, standing, "it's certainly not for the money, and it isn't fun."

"So why?" he asked. "You love me?"

"How about you keep telling yourself that."

"It's how I sleep at night, Mrs. Ross," he said, "dreaming my dreams."

By then, I was knocking on the door. "Bonnie," I said, knocking again, "Bonnie, it's me. It's Mel. Open up, Bonnie."

More silence, and when I looked over my shoulder, Jack was nodding for me to go ahead. I took the key, and in the quiet hallway, we heard the turn and click of it unlocking, and I opened the door.

Bonnie didn't move or say anything, sitting in a chair directly in front of me. She just looked up at me, and I saw that there were no more tears and that she was dried up and empty, her eyes puffy slits. Her hair was up and all over the place, like petals on a sunflower. It spooked me thinking of her staring at the door the whole time, moving the chair right in front of it, and I wondered if she'd heard us talking. "All right," I said, and I went to her, lifted her and directed her to sit at the bed.

I was relieved because she didn't smell like gin and the room smelled gin-less too. It was all body odor, stuffy with grief and sweat, and I opened the window a crack to help. She still wore her track outfit, and I shuffled around in the dresser drawer, looking for her nightgown, saying, "All right now, all right, that's better, let's get you to bed," as if talking to a child. Then I remembered that she was almost a child, only seventeen, and there was no more anger inside me.

When I pulled off her shirt, I saw that she had used her fingernails to make tiny red scratches all up and down her torso, and I said, "Oh, that's not good, Bonnie," and I moved her into the bathroom, set her on the toilet. But it made sense to me, cutting yourself a little to help let the pain out, just a little, where no one could see. I welled up with sadness for her, and for life making no sense. I wet a towel and washed her scratches, and she just sat there in her unhappiness and let me.

"You okay in there?" came Jack's voice from the other room.

I told him to make himself comfortable and that we'd be out in a minute. We heard him shuffling around and settling, and then he said, "Ah hell, Bonnie. I'm so sorry. I'm so goddamned sorry you didn't get to run."

Bonnie looked down a long minute, and then her face met mine with a sad, puzzled expression and she said, "I messed up."

I nodded, for there was nothing to say, and I crouched beside her and took her into my arms. She stayed there for a long time, and finally said into my hair, "I don't cry, Mel, never, never. I never cry, never, never, not even when my momma died, and not even at her funeral," and I said that she made up for lost time, and there was no shame in that, but that she needed to pull it together now for her team. We held each other some more, and a giant heat came from her skin and my body was cool and they merged and turned warm.

When she was done, we pulled apart. I handed her the night-gown and she turned from me, unhooking her brassiere. She pulled the nightgown over her head, and when it was on, she slid her bloomers off and scooted them away from her with a foot. The whole time, she sat at the toilet, maneuvering her clothing, and then she asked if I cried when my momma died. I told her that I was a believer in tears and tried to cry at least once a week to help drain the sadness inside me, and that got a smile from her, a very small sad one, but I saw it and knew that she'd be okay then. I stayed crouched, stroking and taming her wild hair, and she bent forward just a little to give me better access. She said that even when she was a little girl, she'd go crazy when she didn't win. That she could never do anything halfway, and no one could change that about her. She knew that it would be more fun the other way, she said, but she didn't want to do anything unless she could do it better than everyone else. "It's my dream to win gold," she said. "To be the best out of so many millions at one thing."

"Maybe now," I said, "you'll think different. Maybe now, you won't measure yourself in terms of winning and losing," but she just stared at me.

We found Jack sitting at the foot of the bed, his right ankle up and on his left knee. "Ah, hell," he said when he saw us, his foot slipping from his knee to the floor, "Bonnie, I'm so god-damned sorry," and he stood then, taking his turn at holding her. She surrendered to his embrace, and when it was all over, she said, "Who won?" and we told her the American girl, Becky Something-or-other, pretending not to know her last name, and Bonnie groaned and said, "Oh gawd, why'd it have to be her?" because we hated the Americans, entitled and refusing the pension, instead living large on their ship. Rumor had it that they ate ice cream every night, and no one liked them because they just *assumed* they would win. Overcoached, overtrained, overfed, and overconfident, was how Jack put it.

Bonnie said, "When you hear it isn't whether you win or lose but how well you play the game, it just doesn't make sense." She paused, scratched her elbow. "Why then," she said, "did I work so hard to win the gold?"

We didn't say anything to that because she had a good point.

"I'm so tired," she said, sitting at the bed, "but I'm afraid to sleep."

"Why?" I asked.

"I tried."

"What happened?"

"Every time," she said, her eyes round with wonderment, "I'm almost there, almost asleep, and I hear the gun and *boom!* I start running and then I realize what happened."

"Here," Jack said, reaching inside his jacket, "I've got a solution." Then he changed his mind. "Nah," he said, "I want you to do something for me." He pointed to the little desk with the pension stationery and pen tray, and he said, "Take a sheet of that paper and write out a contract, saying that . . ." he paused, looked at me, "saying that—"

"Saying 'I, Bonnie Brody, will not break down in public,'" I said. "'I will save that for private, and I will be there for my team.'"

"And then sign it," Jack said, and Bonnie was already at the desk, the pen scratching across the paper.

She signed and then said, "Done."

Jack came to the desk and read silently, then folded the paper and tucked it in his pocket. He sat at the chair, and Bonnie came and sat beside me at the bed. I scooted and motioned for her to lie down under the covers, and she did. Soon she was asleep, breathing heavily, and we turned off the light and Jack left the room. I stayed and slept in Flo's bed.

But before that happened, Bonnie said, "You want to know something?" and Jack said, "Of course," and she said, "We were talking, all of us, me and Ginger and Flo and Farmer. We played this game where we had to say what scared us most in the world. Flo and Farmer said that they were afraid of death, and I said that I was afraid of losing. Ginger said that she wasn't afraid of death and losing at all, that she was afraid of going crazy. Farmer got this look, and I asked her what she was thinking, but she wouldn't tell me."

She'd been staring straight ahead while she talked, but now she looked from me to Jack and back to me.

"Now," she said, "I know."

"All right," said Jack, "tell us."

"Farmer knew," she said, and she closed her eyes.

"Knew what?" asked Jack. "I don't understand."

But I did, so I answered for Bonnie, who kept her eyes closed. "Based on their fears," I said, "Farmer knew that Bonnie wouldn't win, and that Ginger will," and it seemed obvious to me then that failure had been Bonnie's focus, while Ginger had a foothold on victory, an intimate of inspiration and insanity.

II

I was light-headed from lack of sleep and from soothing egos, helping with meals, dispensing advice, listening to Jack. He felt responsible for what was happening and what was going to happen, the after looming before the now, knowing that the girls had all sorts of things in store, because he'd brought them to Amsterdam and it was history breathing on us.

So I went from my room and was down the hall, and I was thinking about Onata Green saying that you don't know a person until you know how that person wins.

That morning Farmer had paused, the javelin lifted and resting on her hip. Not only had she cut the sleeves from her jersey, her bloomers were cinched to her thighs with elastic bands. There she stood, javelin bolstered, gearing up for her third and final throw. The javelin was so heavy—none of the equipment moderated for females—each time, she poked herself near her shoulder blade on her back, raising a purple-red welt.

When she took off down the runway in long strides, I saw the angel, that profundity in motion that Wallace and I had talked about, her muscles working in beautiful reciprocity, and I, an unbeautiful watcher, felt it singing and working through me.

The flesh on the backs of her thighs contracted and her arm pulled back, slinging the javelin while rotating. I stood along with all the others, knowing something was about to happen, inside the something.

Her hand slipped—an audible intake of breath from us, her audience—but she regained her grip, kept running, and we breathed again. Then she hurled the spear toward her imaginary prey. Her forward momentum made her hop on her right foot to regain her balance.

The stick flew—going—going—a long trajectory—a low needling humming arc—past the flags marking her other throws—still going—past the second- and first-place throws—spinning and soaring—descending and spearing the turf. There it twitched angrily, as though saying, *Take that*, and granting her a gold.

Later she said to me, "This is nothing but fun. And if it ever gets to the point where it isn't, I'll quit."

"How does it feel," I asked, "to be the best?"

"I just beat everybody who showed up today," she said. "How about the gal somewhere in Africa? But she isn't here. She could lick me. Forget about being the greatest in the world. I just beat the ones who got to show up."

I kept walking from my room, and I got to the sisters' room, paused to listen to the burst of noise from inside. Ginger picking and strumming her ukulele. It was only sound, but then there was a recognizable tune, "The Charleston," and there was Ginger laughing, and Flo and Bonnie laughing and clapping, and Danny telling her, Keep going, that's good!

I listened with my ear to the door for a man's voice or laugh, but there was none, so I decided not to knock, and kept walking until I was beyond their noise.

I passed by Farmer's room and paused to listen, since I hadn't heard her in the sisters' room with the girls. At first there was nothing but quiet, and I was just about to leave, but then there was a laugh and it wasn't a regular laugh. It was throaty and full of gratification, and after the laugh came a long soft low moan, and as I listened, my face and body grew warm, because that's the way a woman sounds when someone touches and pleasures her intimately.

For a moment, I was genuinely confused, not knowing what to do, because the person who was laughing wasn't Farmer but was a woman, and there weren't any men to boot from the room. But I was the chaperone.

So I knocked, believing that it was my job, but as soon as my knuckles hit the wood of her door, I felt that I'd made a mistake, and wished that I'd left them alone.

There was quiet for a long time, and I stood frozen and silent, and I knew that they were inside, frozen and silent and waiting, and then finally, the door cracked open an inch or so, and there was Farmer's face very close to mine.

"Oh," she said, relieved to see me instead of someone else, yet there was still something like fear in her face, and it resonated deep inside me.

"I shouldn't have disturbed you," I said, and her face calmed a good deal, and she said, "That's okay, Mel. We're just celebrating my gold." She smiled and said, "You're all red-faced," and I smiled back at her, but it must have been a strange and sad and shamed smile, because she said in a comforting tone, "Really, Mel, I mean it, it's okay," and then she closed the door gently, and I stood there alone.

I tried to let everything settle inside me, but I was still confused and my body was hot, and it seemed that by standing there, trying to make sense, I was intruding. So I shook everything off, deciding that what had happened and what was happening in that room wasn't my business, and that Farmer was a full-grown woman and not a teenager, and it was time for me to move on.

So I kept on walking, and then I was in the lobby. I hadn't been able to run since the train to Montreal, the restlessness building, and the walking helped, so I kept going, out the lobby door and into the dusk.

I was well down the street when I noticed Jack on the other side, walking with his head down, as if he just happened to be there, except that I knew that he was following me, and sent him a stare to let him know.

He kept his head down, but he knew that I knew and his hands dug further into his pockets.

A bird shuffled and tweeted inside a tree, and I searched the branches arched overhead, leaves black-brown against the sky's dying light, and saw the bird's outline. Hello there, I thought to the bird, and it said hello back with song, and I kept moving, thanking the bird with my thoughts, because the walk was working and the bird was an answer.

After some time, I stopped, closed my eyes for a quick Slip Away, listening to the leaves and the sky, distant car noises, the whirring of bicycles, the tinkling of a bicycle's bell. The air smelled of beer, earth, beef, strawberries, exhaust, and something oily and indescribable.

I got my fill and then I was walking again, moving through a narrow street into a less narrow street and back to a narrow one, winding my way beside a canal, Jack behind me, a flickering confirming glimpse of him, and we walked until we came to the water.

The ornately gabled houses, cafés, and restaurants slammed together along the edge, their shadows glimmering on the surface from the streetlights, along with a thin drifting mist. A boat's horn, and then the boat itself, gliding, flat, and filled with people, everyone quiet as it went past, its lights curling over the currents.

We walked and came to a section as quiet as a graveyard—no wind, no people, no boats—trees hanging over the water, empty brick buildings. I leaned on a railing and looked across the canal. Jack leaned next to me. I gathered and gargled saliva, spat into the water, a *plop*. Silly and crass, all for effect.

But Jack said nothing, as if he hadn't seen, and he lit a cigarette and handed me his case. I took one. He leaned toward me and I heard the rasp as he struck a match. He held it for my cigarette, and in the flame I wanted to hide, feeling vulnerable, and that he could see inside me, and that that was why he'd put the light there in the first place. But then he flicked the match dead and I was hidden again.

Smoke coiled and disappeared from our mouths. I could barely hear the suck and lap of the water against the sides. I was thinking that he could ask me questions. Afraid that he would ask, but at the same time keyed up, hoping and wanting him to ask. Wanting to tell him something that I couldn't admit, wanting to admit and tell him at once.

We were quiet for a long time. I got angry, brooding, thinking that none of this was about me. I thought about the noises that came from Farmer's room, and how that wasn't about me, and how this wasn't about me either, and I got angry. I thought about how Jack looked at Ginger sometimes, how all men looked at her, and there was something like jealousy inside me.

Jack had a habit of edging as close as possible to Coach Sacks, and he and Sacks would watch Ginger when she practiced, making themselves invisible, occasionally calling out instructions. Ginger would only look back at them with a blank confidence. She didn't care whether they looked or not. She was good, and she knew she was good, and she didn't need their looks and coaching to confirm it.

A cold breeze swept along the canal. The water sparkled from the streetlights, as though winking at the sky.

I didn't look at Jack but he was looking at me. I could sense him looking.

I tipped my head back and watched the dark blue dome of the sky shivering with stars, and a sagging disappointment filled inside me, believing that none of this was about me.

It wasn't until later that I realized that maybe Jack had followed me to be absorbed with me in silence, and that I hadn't understood.

But that night my blood got hot, rising inside me, and I looked at Jack and said, "You want me to convince Ginger to give her image to your franchise. Convince her to become the Dream Girl for you."

He said nothing, staring into the dark canal.

I coughed, found my breath, sucked in smoke and exhaled.

"Don't blame me," he said, looking up.

I squinted in confusion.

"Don't blame me," he continued, "for the way the world works." His face was a dark gleam, his eyes and nostrils darker gleams.

"Look," he said, "the others, they're going to be okay, but her, I don't know. There's something about her, I don't know—makes me worry."

"She's a grown woman," I said. "She can—"

"Yeah, yeah," he interrupted, for he didn't want to talk, and it wasn't until later that I understood that it wasn't about his plans, or the Dream Girl, or any of that.

He took my arm and guided me, and we walked for an hour or more in silence, until we came to a lit-up tavern, and we went inside and drank beer and listened to the small band. A group of Germans in a corner waved, figuring out who we were, and one of them went to the band and spoke to the leader.

The band struck up "The Maple Leaf Forever." They played it six times for Farmer's gold, and each time, the group of Germans came to attention in the corner, standing stiff and formal in our honor.

The next morning, we had some free time and the girls were feeling homesick, so the girls and I decided to go into town. Farmer and I didn't talk about what had happened, and we never did. The ease between us wasn't disturbed. On the street, there was this little old man—he must have been eighty—with eyebrows like white feathers, and one ear that stuck out of his head like a cauliflower. He put us all in his carriage and said he wanted to show us something in the art museum. So he drove us into town, and he was excited, and we got happy. I didn't think the girls would be interested in an art museum, but they were.

When we got there, the driver escorted us inside, had us put our hands over our eyes, and then he took us to one painting. "Look," he said, and we did. It covered the entire wall. Rembrandt's *Night Watch*. It was staring us back in the face, and we just kept staring at it for a long time. I had seen pictures of paintings in books, but it was alive on the wall, all movement and noise, shadows and light, and a golden girl near the center. Something about the painting put us all in a quiet mood but it wasn't sad or heavy. We had never seen anything like it before. We spent the rest of that morning into the afternoon looking at art, and everyone forgot about being homesick.

III

Sam Sacks lettered in three sports at the University of Toronto— hockey, track, and baseball. A natural but he squandered his talents because of indolence, nights out, women, booze, and cigarettes. But he was such a natural that it was difficult to squander them completely. He ran the 800-metres and at twenty-two was on his way to the Olympics when he got drunk in broad daylight and fell down the front stairs of a bar, breaking his right leg in several places and cracking four ribs.

After that, his life filled with drunken-wasted years. He took a morbid pride in his failures, joining the ranks of bar regulars who delight in their separation from outwardly successful, simpleminded people. A reverse-snobbish camaraderie based on disappointments and the temptation and trap of a catastrophic existence.

Then one afternoon much the same as the others, with Sacks settled at his barstool, a fellow patron near him lifted a newspaper, shoved his finger at the photo of the three women crossing the finish tape of a race, their chests thrust forward and faces strained with the usual mouth-gaping crazed look.

The patron thrust his finger more, finally opining, "Now what the hell makes a girl go and do something stupid like that?"

"I don't know," said Sacks. He stared at the photo, remembering the sucked-in, haunted look he had in the old photos of him mid-run, and then he stared into his forever-diminishing glass of whiskey, pondering some more.

After some time, he looked up and said, "What the hell makes men run, jump, tackle each other, throw a ball, lift weights?"

"Not the same," the other man insisted.

A heated discussion ensued concerning the absurdities of sports, life, motivations, and the sexes. Abruptly, the discussion turned to imaginary exaggerated personal observations of the other's mother and sisters. This dialogue was soon silenced with fisticuffs, ending with both men thrown out of the bar and to the sidewalk.

The fight continued in the dirt outside the bar, a wrangling dust-ball of two, until the authorities came and dragged the men to jail.

It was soon after this fight, while inside a jail cell yet again, awaiting his release for his eleventh drunk-and-disorderly, that

Sacks underwent a mysterious internal psychic shift. Ten years from his career-ending accident, he stopped drinking, smoking, and carousing and took up coaching.

There weren't many willing to coach girls, even though Sacks later claimed they listened better, so it was only a matter of time for Jack to find him, and Jack paid him well enough.

The underdog status of girls was a definite lure, but Coach Sacks also took satisfaction in knowing that no matter how hard the girls trained or tried, they would never be as fast as he was in his prime, and he told them so on a regular basis. He insisted that this information motivated them, even after I told him that it motivated him.

When stationary, Coach Sacks still looked like an athlete: tall, broad-shouldered, solid. But when he moved, his shoulders pulled forward and he walked with a dragging limp. He stayed still as much as possible, leaned against fences and walls.

Unlike most coaches, he didn't yell. He rarely raised his voice. His heart had weakened from his destructive years, and he was careful to maintain his composure. But there was also a quiet ease and calm that came from his having used up his stupidity and loud brashness in the bars.

He treated the girls with respect and they responded. He was in his mid-thirties and they were young, so that I was not that surprised when he and Flo developed an intense connection, as she was training for the 800-metres, his race that he lost without ever running. He trained with her the longest: Jack brought them together before Ginger, Farmer, and Bonnie.

Flo demanded his attention and took pride in messing with his impartiality. There was between them a familiarity suggestive of marital unselfconsciousness and emotional telepathy, yet Coach Sacks was also indulgent of her like a besotted father. Attentive, cautious, and watchful, he was disturbed by her flirtations with other men, which were frequent. But she came back to him for support, and he was her center.

He taught her to run as he had, and he'd lean against the wall and watch her, an echo of him. Before she met him, she had just been running, something she did, a race here and there, most she won, some she lost. He taught her to go faster, take longer strides, hold her head higher, to use more arm action, to keep her elbows closer to her sides. She joked that he hypnotized her, and he did have blazing eyes, hardly ever blinking, just staring through you, burning away.

He told her that it wasn't the first lap but the second and final lap that was the farthest from the finish. The 800-metres was lost on that second lap, records broken or forfeited, careers made or ended. A small space between anonymity and fame, greatness and mediocrity, happiness and despair. The second lap wasn't a metaphor for life, he said, but for every bad thing you endured and continued to endure.

The others ran clumsily, heads back, arms flinging, and all effort. Her running was assured, distance combined and measured with speed, all grace. He knew her inside and out, and that was why when he said, "Keep her from distractions," I knew that he was telling me to keep her away from the boys.

Bonnie was enlisted in this task, as she was Flo's roommate. Both girls were in high school. And though Flo behaved like a high school girl, Bonnie did not. Ever since her disqualification, Bonnie was responsible, helpful, trustworthy, and my personal spy. She was beginning to understand that if running was the only thing in her life, if it was her only purpose, then when she lost, she had no other purpose. For her, losing was devastating, but now that she'd lost, she had to do a lot of soul-searching.

When Bonnie knocked on my door after breakfast that morning, saying, "It's me," I knew before opening it that Flo was in trouble and that most likely this trouble included a boy.

As I followed Bonnie to the track, she explained that Flo was practicing with some of the boys and that maybe she was overreacting, maybe that was okay, but that she didn't know for sure. I told her that she'd done the right thing by coming to get me. Flo's greatest weakness was the inability to ignore a dare, especially when boys were involved.

A warm foggy rain drifted down, and I said, "Her heat's tomorrow," and Bonnie said, "I told her to stay put," and I said, "She's just warming up, it's probably okay," and Bonnie said, "Sure," but we both knew how competitive Flo was, and how she liked to show off.

We got there and saw Flo running calmly alongside the boys' 1,500-metre runner, Scotty Walter, and they were talking casually. Bonnie and I looked at each other and laughed in relief.

Scotty and Flo continued running, and we stood watching and waiting for them to make their way to our side of the track. Scotty was lean, with the narrow face and loping stride of a greyhound, and his dark hair flopped into his eyes.

I looked up into the sky for a second, feeling the mist but not seeing it, and then, "Oh no," I heard Bonnie say, "no, no, no," and my eyes met her horrified face and followed her gaze to Scotty, speeding to pass Flo.

Flo sped up too, not wanting Scotty to pass, and then he went faster, and so did she, and I yelled, "No!" but before we could do anything, Flo was full-out racing Scotty and he was full-out racing her.

They were headed toward us, their faces full of strain and determination from going all out, and then he was looking over his shoulder, for she was behind him a few paces, and she went down in a running somersault.

My hand was over my mouth and Bonnie's hand was over hers, and then we were running to Flo's crumpled fetal-like body, hearing her agonized groan. She went to a sit, pulling her knee to her chest, and the first thing she said was, "Don't tell Sacks."

But with his radar-like Flo alert, Coach Sacks sensed something, for there he was, hobbling in a wide step with incredible speed across the track, his arms swinging, helping to propel him. He looked like a great bumbling ostrich. His eyes were fixed on us, his face red. He made his way sideways between two boys, pushing and dodging, and then he was in the clear, crossing toward us again.

Scotty, Bonnie, and I opened a space from our huddle, and Coach Sacks inserted himself, taking over in an awkward kneeling position. He lifted and assessed Flo's leg, angled her foot, tested its ankle.

"A muscle strain," he said in a calm tone, "not bad. We'll ice it, and you'll be fine." His assurance, however, did not correspond with his worried expression.

We were quiet, and I wished for the great relief of the day's inking itself to night, of the whiskey rattling in my flask and then tilting and moving from flask to lips to mouth to throat to heart.

And then Coach Sacks broke the silence along with his magnanimity: "What in the hell were you thinking?" His eyes were wet and partly closed. "Goddamn Jesus Christ!"

Flo said, "Sorry! I'm so sorry! It was so stupid," and her eyes, usually bold and reckless, were full of remorse.

With gravitas, Scotty apologized, and there was nothing more to say but Coach Sacks said, "I'm at a loss. I can think of nothing that fills me with greater loathing than a display of stupidity for stupidity's sake."

Flo looped an arm around Bonnie and Scotty and was hop-stepped back to her room, where she rested and iced her muscle, and prayed to be ready in the morning for her 800-metre heat.

But before we left her room, Coach Sacks looked at her in bed, and he kept looking so that she couldn't take it.

"Anyway," she said, hesitantly, wildly, watching him closely, "it was an accident." She gripped his arm. "Anyway," she continued, "there's more to life."

Coach Sacks shook his arm free. He stared at Flo in disbelief.

"I mean," said Flo, "well, life goes on."

"Sure," said Coach Sacks, but he meant the opposite.

"You fell," she said, "you fell worse than what I did."

"I did," agreed Coach Sacks, looking down at her.

The following morning was warm and overcast and needed to rain. The sleeves of my dark-blue dress were flecked with tiny drops of moisture but the specks disappeared seconds after arrival, and when I reached out my hand, I felt nothing. So the rain swelled in the sky and didn't release, and the girls gathered for the 800-metre heat.

Farmer agreed to run with Flo for moral support, even if she wasn't a long-distance runner, and there they were, jogging side by side to the starting line, running in such beautiful synchronicity that they looked for a moment like twins.

Flo's leg hurt but Coach Sacks wrapped it earlier, telling her if she could get right mentally, that would help. "Don't try to pass anyone," he said. "Pull up behind and then cut out fast. Unleash the entire sprint you got toward the finish. Cut out around and get your lead and cut in again, fast, before anyone knows what's going on. If someone tries to pass, listen to her stride and don't look back. Listen and guess. Just when you think she's going to begin sprinting, lengthen out and pull away. Don't let the runners know you're in a hurry. You can overtake them without letting them know."

Flo nodded and Coach Sacks took his pocket watch, lifted it and said, "What's this?"

"My enemy."

"What are you going to do?"

"Conquer it."

So everyone agreed that Farmer would help with the mental, and Farmer was jiggling her fingers, and Flo was jumping up and down. A few of the runners were running back and forth in their lanes.

The slow terrible minutes came before the race—drawing for positions, instructions imparted, and the awful hush before the starter's commands. Then Flo was digging her feet in the dirt and looking over at Farmer, six girls down, and Farmer was looking back, digging her feet and nodding, yes, I'm here, Flo, you're okay. Flo looked ahead, concentrated, fingers sprawled in front of her, shoulders down.

There was a calm in the midst of the commotion. A single instant of composed disbelief that it was about to happen, in a fraction of a second, it would happen, after the months, the miles, the mornings, the travel, the practices, finally happening.

Then the gun was fired and a cloud of white smoke rose above the man who'd fired it, and the girls sprang forward in a wave. The pack of girls joggled, loosened, and stretched from each other, like a fist opening into a hand. Coach Sacks leaned at the wall of the stadium next to Jack and cursed aloud while Jack patted his arm.

Flo said later that the noise from the stadium added to the growing roar in her head, and she let it fuel her stride. She started strong and moved into it, building her speed, forgetting her pain, her legs unconnected. For an instant, she looked over a lane and saw Farmer staring right back, and it got her feet to fly even more.

The second lap, her mouth went dry. She felt nothing but pain and torment running toward the tape, the faces of the crowd blending and swimming as if she were in a dream. Behind her was the tenacious ghost-sound of feet chasing her, urgent and alarming, gaining, but she reached the tape before the sound caught up. She clenched her fist high above her head as she crossed, and then the American girl crossed. Third came Farmer, to everyone's surprise, qualifying her.

A few of the girls went to their knees after the race, and I watched the reporters scribbling. A pair collapsed at the field, lying at their backs looking up at the sky, and their hands went to each other. They kept holding hands, staring up at the sky, and I wanted to tell the reporters that they had it all wrong.

The American girl was found to have been paced by a team-mate on the infield, an infraction worthy of disqualification, but the authorities chose to overlook it, issuing a mere warning. Bonnie said, "Why'd I get disqualified, and she gets nothing?" and the only answer we could come up with was that she was American.

Nine runners, including Farmer and a bandaged Flo, lined up for the 800-metre final the following afternoon.

I accompanied Farmer for her warm-up beforehand, and Flo stayed in her room and rested her leg, hurting from the strain of the 800-metre heat the day before. The noise from the stadium barely carried to us on the outside, at a plot of grass where no one went. Farmer did her stretches, her easy jog, some sprints. The clamor in her head needed to be contained, unleashed only in the ferocity surrounding the pistol crack. Now the buildup floated inside her. Grief, despair, worry, the tension of her body. Building to release until there was nothing left.

Trying to warm up in the stadium, being too close to the crowds, made the girls frazzled, causing the buildup to come in gushes, getting them there too early or ending it too soon. It was better to warm up in private, in quiet, in comfort, this last bit of calm. Though Farmer wanted me there and asked me to come, she didn't speak the entire time.

Once we entered the stadium with its circus-like atmosphere, Farmer said to me, "I can hardly swallow," and I told her that she would be okay, that once she got moving she would know it was like all the other times, that the noise inside and around her would be drowned out by her legs running.

The crowd went wild over something, and we both shot looks around us, and it was no longer privacy but all jolt, all electric and connected.

The girls positioned in their concentrated squat-like prayerful places at the starting line. Eighteen legs attached to nine bodies, nine hearts, poised and waiting, that tiny calm second of forever before the gun.

Jack stood with Coach Sacks, and Coach Sacks reached up and fumbled with his collar, jerking the button and tie loose. His head was going from side to side as if stretching the muscles.

Then there was the burst of the pistol shot, and Flo rose like a bird from the starting line, Farmer just behind. There was that familiar second of shocked silence from the crowd and then it erupted. Farmer was near Flo but by the first half Flo was running a close third, and Farmer was toward the end.

At the beginning of the second lap, Flo was passed by the Swedish girl. Flo recharged, overtaking a German girl and holding her position as she neared the final stretch. Then the Japanese girl surged, drawing even, and she swung an arm, accidentally striking Flo, knocking her off stride. The collision shook Flo's concentration. She was fading, with the American girl closing in.

Farmer saw what was happening, and she darted and passed four runners, and it was the most remarkable and purest piece of sportsmanship I ever saw. My shout was lost in the noise of the crowd, and my heart wanted to leap through my skin and hop on the ground in front of me. Farmer drew even with Flo and coaxed her to go all out. Flo responded, her leg shooting out a little further, and then she was back to her great leaping strides. It was as if Farmer was holding her. Connected as they neared the finish, linked like a web, their sweat one and the same, and their breath, and then a hesitation in Farmer, a falling back, allowing Flo to cross before her.

At the finish, Farmer placed her arm on Flo's shoulder, they took a few steps, and Flo dropped—knees to hands—down to the ground. Farmer went beside her, comforting and consoling, her arms around her, and I knew in that deep place inside me that Farmer could've finished fourth, or even higher, but that she believed that this was Flo's race. She was there to support Flo, not to beat her, and so that was what she did. Then Farmer looked up and gave me one dazed, confirming glance.

Three girls collapsed on the infield and cried, including Flo, and first aid was rushed to them, the reporters writing about how women weren't up to the Olympics, look at them, hysterical and exhausted. But there wasn't anything wrong. The girls living a moment they couldn't believe existed, needing to lie on the ground to take it all in. Both creators and beneficiaries of history, and it was confusing and overwhelming, and they needed to lie down and cry as the moment exploded.

But the reporters kept writing, and the officials rushed to administer first aid. The scene of the girls in need after the 800-metres was enough for the all-male International Amateur Athletic Federation to ban girls from all races longer than 200-metres. One of the officials said, "The effect and fatigue of competition does not conform to the ideals of womanly dignity and conduct. It doesn't lead to the promotion of sport, but on the contrary, because of its effects on the spectators, is detrimental."

The rule holds and most likely will be there when I'm dead and gone. I've come to understand that distance running, more than any other event, is the great equalizer. You don't have to have good equipment or expensive tracks or coaches, and it just doesn't matter. But they're making sure to keep us out.

We run because we choose to run. The 800-metres, the 1600-metres, a marathon, and you can choose, and that makes the difference. But they're saying no, it's not our choice. As if they know what's best.

It reminds me of a person bringing a treat right up close to a doggie's mouth—the doggie smelling, jumping, and opening its jaws—and the person pulling the treat away, saying, no, no, that's enough, you've had enough, you're just a doggie.

That afternoon, the girls collapsed and cried, and it was used against us, and when Flo was done, she asked me to walk with her from the stadium to our pension and pretend that we were in conversation. She didn't want to have to talk to anyone or hear anyone say how great her race was or how she deserved a medal and almost got the bronze. So we walked, but no one spoke to us, and the sun was down, the sky a silvery mist that faded from pale blue to steel gray. It turned out that when we entered the lobby, everyone scattered, pretending that they didn't see us or know us, because they didn't want to discuss what had happened either.

Before we started back, Flo sat in a chair and Coach Sacks stood with his head bent over her. The tears were coming from Flo, and Coach Sacks said, "You broke your record. You've got no reason to cry. I'm proud of you. You've got nothing to be ashamed about," and I loved him for it. But she couldn't see, hear, or feel—disappointment and regret all over her—reducing her accomplishments to what she could have done, would have done, might have done, should have done.

I had a flashing premonition, understanding that Flo would distance herself from Farmer, because Farmer's generosity in those seconds was a reminder. Coach Sacks would ask Flo to marry him, but she would say no. She wanted to win more than she knew, even more than she wanted to win for Coach Sacks, and now he was a reminder. She would marry eventually, and that man would be the opposite of Coach Sacks, who would never marry.

I thought of Virginia Woolf and her vision of generations interlinked and minds "threaded together . . . this common mind that binds the whole world together; and all the world is mind." And I saw Flo as an old woman after a quiet life, no more competitions, not talking about the Olympics, her grandchildren asking questions, getting little from her.

IV

I walked the streets near the pension that night, turning the day over in my mind until it lost some of its heaviness, moving through cobbled routes with bars and restaurants, and passing a dark alley where two couples embraced along the wall. Why so many lovers in Amsterdam? In public, waiting for passersby. In Toronto, the lovers tend toward privacy. Maybe I was noticing them more and it was the same everywhere. Nevertheless, no one could stop me or tell me that it was unsafe, so I walked.

I thought about the 400-metre relay race to come and Ginger's high jump, and there was nothing to do but to stop and look up at the stars and the tilted glowing smile of a moon and pray. Yes, I reached that stage, composing a prayer-letter:

Dear God, I know You've got more important matters but it would mean a great deal to the girls, and to me . . .

I believe in the nebulous, indefinable, and preferable I-Don't-Know, connected to the void and easily mistaken as failure or losing. Yet there I was, staring up into the night, where the preachers had told me that God lived, pining for the unambiguous ego-boost assurance of victory.

When I was done talking to God or myself or to the sky or all three, I didn't know, and listening, for that time I waited for God to say something back, though I knew from childhood experience that God didn't believe in talking direct, I continued on walking.

The shutters were closed on the houses, here and there a clink of light and the sound of voices, and when I reached the canal, a lamppost reflected and glimmered its rays on the water. I thought about Ginger. The photographers surrounded her all the time now. How strange to have strangers think that they know you, love you, and desire you, without ever meeting you, all the while being so young and not even knowing yourself.

Back at the pension, I settled at the hotel bar for a nightcap, something I'd never done before, for I was still very restless, and the gentleman next to me said, "Do you mind if I smoke?"

"Not at all," I said. He proffered his cigarette case my direction and I said, "No thanks."

We took each other in, the dim light conducive to a more favorable opinion. He was all face with a large caterpillar-like mustache and a gleam of teeth. I don't know what he saw in me, except that my cloche hat was pulled low and I tried for a smile with questionable success.

We were both at the age where the outward fortunes of flesh were overtaken with character. When I noticed a mole on his neck the size of a thimble, repulsion and attraction came over me, both wanting to look away and investigate the dark protrusion further with my fingertips—or my tongue!

"You don't smoke?" he said.

"Not in public," I said, and he laughed.

Without further eye contact, I drank the final dregs of bourbon from my glass, and then set my hand at the bar so that my modest wedding ring was on prominent display.

But it didn't dissuade him.

"Can I buy you another?"

"No."

His caterpillar lip rose in a smile. "Can't I get you anything?"

I played with that suggestion, and then all at once I got hot and angry.

He repeated his query: "Isn't there anything I can get you?"

I looked at him very hard and said, "Nothing that I can have."

The environment didn't encourage nuance, or I must not have conveyed sufficient severity, because he laughed, complimented my wit, raised his hand for the bartender, and ordered us both another round.

I made for my purse to leave and he said, "What's wrong?"

A peal of laughter came from the end of the bar.

"I'm not looking for romance."

"What?" he asked, because I'd surprised him.

So I said it again.

He looked at me for a long moment before saying, "Then you won't find it."

The bartender brought our drinks, and an awkward silence hung in the air.

"Nothing wrong," the man muttered defensively into his glass, "with wanting a little company."

He had a valid point and I sipped at my bourbon, for it seemed wrong to waste it. "Sorry," I said, but he ignored me, keeping his gaze at his glass. His cigarette case was between us, so I slid it toward me, my hand passing his downward vision.

He looked up and I leaned from my bar stool toward him, cigarette propped in my mouth. After a brief, indecisive pause, he lit the cigarette for me.

He was Tom, an assistant coach for the New Westminster Salmon Bellies, the Canadian lacrosse team, and after three more bourbons each, we were close, close friends. So close, in fact, that my hand was on his hard muscular arm, leaning into him to whisper my appreciation after he had whispered his, when I caught in a large smoked mirror behind his head the spectacle of Jack coming through the door of the bar.

My heart leapfrogged to my throat, and I tucked my hand into Tom's armpit, watching from his shoulder. Jack's image hung in the mirror, along with the reflection of lights and bottles.

Jack looked around the bar—kept looking—looking for what? Looking for me?

Sparks of light surrounded him. I swear it. He stood surveying, his eyes going from one side of the bar to the other, haloed in light, and I hid like a coward. Smelling the woodsy smoke of Tom's sleeve while watching Jack, a sweet terror blazed inside me. All magic and love. But I sat with the feeling longer, and it tangled in hate. I hadn't been with a man besides Wallace.

Hiding within another man's pectoral, my belly full of booze and my heart opened, I knew undeniably that it was Jack whom I wanted, and this made me angry. So I continued to look across the bar at Jack looking, and I didn't want it to be true. With all my heart, I didn't want it to be true. But it didn't matter what I wanted. My feelings for Jack were as real to me in that moment as the mole on Tom's neck, which happened to be brushing against my forehead.

I caught a flash of Jack's eyes possibly recognizing me, and I gripped Tom's arm to steady myself at his chest. Tom didn't mind me burrowing into him, and his hands went to my back to prove it, encouraging further nestling.

I did not move or look around or meet Jack's eyes, and then he was beside us. Tom's hands released me, and Jack said, "Mel." I didn't look. "Mel," he said, "come on, it's time to go."

I decided there was no recourse but to meet reality, pulling away from Tom. Jack's face was very serious and worried and it sobered me considerably.

Tom's head went to the side and he said, "Mel?" I'd told him that my name was Mary, probably because of Onata Green's Mary, and that was the last thing Tom said to me, a great big questioning "Mel?" and I never saw his mole, caterpillar mustache, or woodsy-smelling pectorals again.

Jack took my arm and guided me from the bar. When we were a distance away, he said, "That's not like you, Mel. You don't even know that man."

I was sick, as though he'd socked me in the stomach, feeling that I'd betrayed him or me or Wallace or all three of us. Then my sickness changed to anger and I said, "So what?" Further angered by my inelegant rejoinder, I said, "Who cares," and decided to leave it there, as each time I opened my mouth, I was disappointed.

Jack led me toward the hallway. "What about your reputation?" he said, alluding to our conversation on the ship. He stopped and stared heavily into my face, and I put my hand out to touch him.

"Oh, Jack," I said, grasping him by the arm. "My reputation?" Then I lowered my head and released the bourbon from my stomach onto his pants and shoes.

I woke in the morning and sat at the side of my bed, my feet on the cold floor and the taste of cigarettes, bourbon, and vomit at the back of my tongue, wearing the same dress as the night before, and my cloche hat. My dream was still with me, a twisting uphill race, a pack of women and men, and me running behind them. I watched the increasing nearness of their bloomers—for some reason, that was all I could see, and both the men and the women wore red bloomers—until I came upon them. They were bouncing up and down, and then I was bouncing with them and gradually moving beyond them. But then there were more in front of me, and I approached them individually and went past, and then another, and I went past, and they kept springing up like trees. I kept passing them easily, every one—as if they were standing still—but they kept on coming. Then everything grew dark because we were running in a forest. All of us sliding downward, winding around, faster and faster. I tried to break from the pack but I couldn't. It was impossible. The runners pounded on all sides of me and I couldn't move.

I was in a great downhill stride, my feet smashing, and then the elbow of the person next to me struck my side, and for an instant I continued to run wildly, arms waving for balance, and I went down running. I rolled down a hill, hitting things as I went, striking against Ginger's ukulele and her rag doll, and I was falling more and more, and then I finally landed beneath a small wooden footbridge. I lay on my side listening to the thunder of legs passing overhead, the rustle and muffled reverberations of their feet on the wood, and they galloped past me and then were gone. But I waited for the stragglers, and two more came, their feet clumping over me, and then they were gone. I looked and saw the spine of earth showing through the grass where their feet had tread, the soil printed with thousands of shoes, and then I woke.

I sat there and waited for the dream to leave me, and then I was remembering Jack helping me to bed, a growing searching look in his eyes mixed with a deep concern, and that was enough to confuse and embarrass me. I didn't want to remember more, so I roped off everything that had transpired into a remote section of my brain. It would have to sit and wait to be thought about further, when I could manage better.

Later while I bathed, the cordoned section of Jack helping me to bed and what had happened reared forth, and I thought about all the things I might have said, and of those things I might have said, what among them that I most wanted to say, and then the impossibility of ever saying any of them.

My hands trembled when I got dressed, and every now and then I had to steady myself with a long breath. I drank two cups of coffee and ate a poached egg with a slice of toast, and then I was back to being me.

V

The girls won the gold for the 400-metre relay. Bonnie crossed the yarn neck-high, clutching the baton at her side, and the force drew a slim scratch of blood across her neck. The girls hopping and hugging and the flashbulbs couldn't make them be still, and that's how I like to remember them. Reporters and photographers yelling *hold still stay still*, and they have their arms around each other, and one looks at the next with unbridled contagious joy, and then they're hopping and hugging again, uncontained.

The following afternoon, it took Ginger ten jumps to win the gold in the high jump, and it wasn't until later that I understood that this was part of the problem. It was all too easy. It was easy and natural and it was the natural act of jumping, and how could a silly thing like jumping that came natural mean so much? Coaches, family, newspapers, the audience wanting to take credit and make it something more, so that she came to distrust.

The New York Times called her the prettiest girl at the Games. Did that make her skills incidental? She wanted it to be about the jumping, but it was more about what she looked like. Secretly, the attention and praise must have made her feel superior, even when she knew that wasn't right. Her beauty, athletic ability, and jumping style undeserving of so much praise and attention, and she never liked or wanted attention, but it also made her superior, and so she hated the results and herself, and she came to distrust.

"Jesus," the boy watching next to me said, in pure admiration, "Jesus, she's gorgeous," and he swallowed hard, having said it all.

Wet, drizzly, and cold, and she didn't remove her warm-up

clothes, scaring her twenty-three opponents, not even needing to remove her warm-ups, because it all came so easy to her and she was making sure to let them know. They thought the crowd was cheering for them, and then Ginger waved and the cheers tripled, swelled and heaved in the air, and I felt it inside me, too. Between jumps, wrapped in a big red Hudson Bay blanket, composed and steely.

Her competitors gradually eliminated, and then there was one jump left to win and three chances, the high jump the paradox event that you win by losing. You jump until you lose or forfeit, but then you've won.

When her foot clipped the standard, knocking down the bar, the warm-ups were removed for her second jump.

Running in a J toward the bar, making her approach, planting her foot, and then she was suspended in the air, a perfect position—not going up, not going down—just hanging there, legs scissored, bloomers and shirt ballooning, and she wasn't just jumping, she was flying.

We all saw her fly. Don't come down, we thought. Don't come down just yet. Hold it. A split second of experiencing perfection. The flashbulbs blazing, and then it was done.

An opportunity to attempt a new world's record of five feet three inches, what she'd already done in her backyard, and her third jump was successful, but there was a sag in the bar. That was happening all the time. They'd say a record was broken, then somebody would make a mistake and then they'd change their minds, saying, Whoops, sorry, maybe next time.

Another opportunity but she was tired and cold and decided that was that.

From obscurity to the most photographed female Olympian in less than two years, with her faraway sadness that came across as poise, all because she was a girl who loved to jump in her backyard.

I've always had a nagging suspicion that sports are ridiculous. Meaningful and meaningless and all the while ridiculous, that equation of which outweighs the other dependent on temperament and perspective. I'd like to believe that sports have meaning more than meaninglessness, and I cherish that hope. But that doesn't mean sports aren't ridiculous.

While in the midst of her own flattering golden realm of being the Dream Girl, Ginger shared my suspicion and lived it.

That night the reporters surrounded the girls in the pension lobby, asking questions, and Ginger stood there blinking, lonely and lost. A crowd of spectators gathered, chanting Dream Girl, Dream Girl, Dream Girl, and she just stood there, blinking. Then she turned to me and I caught a glimpse of confusion—anger—and I knew that she wanted to jam their cheers and questions back down their throats. They loved her but she did not love them, and I could see it. The more they would love her, the more she would hate them. They would love her and she would not love them, and then they would hate her.

Then she turned and made her way down the hallway leaving us, and Danny followed her, and they disappeared. Jack and I hadn't spoken since he'd cleaned my vomit from his shoes, and he was staring at me from across the room, letting me know that I should follow.

I started down the hallway, and Farmer stopped me and asked, "Does she mean it?"

"Mean what?"

"That she doesn't care about winning, or our team, or any of it."

"Did she say that to the reporters?"

"No. Just to me."

"She doesn't mean it."

Farmer nodded thoughtfully. "She's tired," she said. "I don't understand her," she added, and I told her that it wasn't her job.

"But I'm team captain," she said.

I told her that I had to leave, which was true, and I worked my way through the crowd and reporters and down the hallway to the sisters' room.

I knocked and let them know it was just me, so Danny opened the door.

Propped on her bed with her rag doll, Ginger stared at me.

"What you said," I said, "to Farmer. Tonight. You said that you didn't care about the team. Did you mean it?"

She kept on staring, cold and remote.

"You said that?" Danny asked her.

Ginger was quiet and we waited and then she said, "Hugh says it's all hogwash. Winning for flag and country." She was talking about Hugh Williams. He'd won both the 100- and the 200-metres, and now Canada and the world loved him. But he did not love them. He didn't love to run. He didn't even like it. His father left when he was a baby, his coach was a dictator, and his mother was also a dictator, and he won, because that's the way it works sometimes. But he didn't like it.

Ginger turned her eyes from me and stared out the window, where globs of rain trickled down the glass. I decided not to press her further, but it bothered me that she was denigrating her team.

Danny walked me out and we stood in the dark hallway with the door closed. We could hear Ginger plucking at her ukulele, a nonsense song.

"She doesn't mean it," Danny said, and we were both afraid, so we let the words hang there, and neither of us said anything more about it.

Later that night came the fight between Bonnie and Ginger, and I didn't get there until the end. Danny came down the hall to my room. I heard her feet on the floor and then she knocked at my door. I opened the door, started to say hello, but she had my arm and was tugging me before anything came out of my mouth.

"Hurry," she said. "They're gonna kill each other." Her black hair was wild and her face chalk-white. She wore her blue and pink nightgown and her feet were bare, and she ran and held my arm, and I ran but Bonnie and Ginger had already finished their fight by the time we got there, and they were still alive.

What I remember most about that night is the way Ginger looked. In the corner, knees hugged at her chest, a scratch across her cheek. Her eyes weren't flat anymore and I was glad. She seemed alive with anger and hurt, and I must admit that it made me glad.

Across from her stood Bonnie, stunned and flushed and still breathing hard, nose bloodied and a red splotch blooming at her arm.

I stood and looked from Bonnie to Ginger and back again, and then I felt a presence come over the room, as if a large bird were flying over us, darkening the room with its wingspan, and then it was gone.

We like to believe that our lives are in our control. Yet sometimes a jolt knocks us off balance and changes us, determining the course we take for the rest of our lives.

"I told her," Bonnie was saying, "I told her that she's selfish. That she's selfish and that it isn't right. I never liked her. Never. That it isn't right that the one who's selfish gets to win. I told her that she didn't even try her hardest. I could tell. She didn't even try her hardest. The one who doesn't need the luck gets the luck, and why does that happen? It's not right. Then she grabbed my wrist and said that I didn't know what I was talking about. That I don't know what's inside her. I said that I do. That there's nothing but ugliness inside her, and that she has everyone fooled because she's pretty but she hasn't fooled me"—she stopped, took a long breath—"Then she shook me. She shook me and said that she could have any man that she wanted"—she paused again, took another breath—"she said that when we got back to Canada, that she would find Coach Frank, my Coach Frank, and have him. She would have him and think about me and laugh, and that's when I hit her."

"Oh, Ginger," I said, and we all looked at Ginger. "You don't mean that." But she sat there looking back at us like she meant it.

"She . . . ," Bonnie said, and her face contorted with rage, grief, and despair, "she's evil. She's mean and she's evil and she's selfish."

"You don't know me," Ginger said, her voice low. She lifted her chin, turned her eyes on Bonnie. "You don't know anything. Leave me alone."

Bonnie said, "I know something's wrong with you."

Ginger's head went down. We all knew that there was something wrong with Ginger, and our awareness filled the room, and her head just continued to hang down as the saddest kind of proof. She kept it like that for a long while, and then finally Bonnie spoke.

"I'm sorry," she said, and we were all surprised. I wasn't sure if she was apologizing for her part in the fight or for telling Ginger that there was something wrong with her and making it fill up the room, or for both.

I looked at Ginger. She didn't move or speak. She just looked back at me, and I saw that her eyes had tears in them and that she wasn't evil or mean or selfish. But that she was endless. You could open one door to try to find her, only to find another door, and another, and another, endlessly opening the doors inside her and never finding her, even if she wanted to be found. Her psychological inheritance. No matter how she fought, it would capture her.

I felt so sorry for her that I wanted to cry.

Chapter Eight

Good Wife

"Christ," Jack said, sinking onto the couch next to me. We were in his room at the pension. He shoved the newspaper aside, reached up and unbuttoned his collar, fumbled with his tie. He loosened it, pulled it over his head, and flung it across the room where it spun and landed in a snakelike coil beside the desk. "Christ," he said again, peevish, "can't Wallace talk to you in another way?"

The IAAF delegates had met to decide the future of the women's track and field events. Our esteemed Canadian representative—my very own Wallace—had voted against women's future participation, citing previous concerns: that women weren't allowed in the ancient Greek Olympics and that competitive sports were injurious to our health.

"It's a disgrace," Jack said, "a humiliation. A slap in our face. A slap in your face."

"Yes," I said. "I know." I drew my legs beneath me. "We're okay," I reminded him, for only six of the sixteen had voted to ban us.

"That's not the point."

"I know."

"He agrees with the Vatican," he said. "The goddamn Vatican is against us."

"He doesn't mean it."

Jack got up and walked across the room. He stopped in front of the window, thought for a moment. Then he turned to face me.

"Why are you defending him?"

"I'm not," I said, and I was surprised and a little bit awed because I was lying. My feet came to the floor. I feigned casualness, bent toward the table, lit a cigarette, but my fingers trembled.

I leaned back into the couch, tried for relaxation. But it was like Wallace was right there, breathing on me. Sending his message across the ocean, letting me know that he was desperate, crazy, and our situation dire. A public declaration and bid to control me through his position, and instead of anger, there was a ball of tenderness rolling around inside me, shot through with sorrow, and it made no sense.

"You're defending him," Jack said, and he paced across the carpet, swung past me, and paced again.

I stubbed the cigarette around in the ashtray, watching it die.

"Making excuses," he said. There was a bowl of ice, soda water, and a bottle of Scotch and he made me a drink, and then a much bigger one for himself. "How do you think it makes the girls feel? Winning for Canada, and then Canada votes against them."

"Lousy," I said.

"Disappointed," he added. "Angry. Betrayed." He held the glass out to me. "Take it," he said, and I did.

"If you were a good wife," he said, "he would have voted for us."

"You have a wonderful sense of humor," I said.

"It's your fault," he said. He paused, thinking. "I don't under-stand," he said, shaking his head, and then he gave me a big heap of silence. He floundered in the quiet for a while and then he said, "I don't understand women. At all." Another pause. "Let's take you, for instance."

"Let's not," I offered.

"You make him your authority."

"How about," I suggested, "you don't talk about things that you know nothing about."

But he was on a roll. "Oh, please," he said in a baby voice, pressing his palms together in prayer position, "approve of me. You're the boss. You make the rules."

There was nothing to say to that absurdity.

"I'm trying to make a point," he said.

"It's complicated."

"Suppose so," he said. "It's a goddamn wonder, is what it is."

He sank down next to me and drank from his glass, one leg drawn up on the knee of the other, all the time staring at me. He kept on looking and not talking. Thinking and accusing in his stare, and I met his gaze back for a while but it tired me out, and I decided to investigate the carpet pattern.

I drank the last of my drink and handed my empty to him. He reached and took it, not taking his eyes off me, and set it on the table.

He said very solemn and quiet: "You still love him."

"No," I said, even though I didn't know, and even more I didn't know how to tell Jack that I didn't know, so I settled for what came easy.

"You do," he said, and he took me by my arms and drew me toward him. His eyes glittered with need and hurt, and he drew me even closer so that his breathing was on my cheek.

"You still love him," he whispered, and his words traveled through my ear and piled up in my throat like I'd said them, and I didn't pull back.

But he did. Then he shifted and turned, lying on his back with his head in my lap and his legs and feet hanging over the edge of the couch. He put my hand on his chest, and I played at a button of his shirt, my other hand on his forehead. He moved my fingers from his forehead so that they covered his eyes. For a long time we didn't talk. I kept my hand over his eyes, and the heat came from him and moved through me, and I didn't know what to do.

So I closed my eyes and kept my hands on Jack. But it was Wallace whom I saw, sitting in his chair before his desk, his arms laid out. Something pathetic about him, a mini-god with his fragile arrogance and audacity. I wasn't sure if what I felt was love or sympathy for his weaknesses. It seemed to me then that a lot of men shared these traits, and that I loved them, too.

Despite Jack's heavy head in my lap, I had a sense of dissolving, as if I'd been blown by the wind and was now suspended in the air without shape. So I opened my eyes, came back into my body.

Jack removed my hand from his face.

"I know that you don't feel the same way about me," he said. He looked serious, staring up at me.

"What?"

"That's fine," he said. "I'm fine with that. Really. I'm actually okay with the way things are."

"Excuse me," I said.

"I deserve it."

"I don't understand."

"I'm saying," he said, "that I can live with it."

I felt hot as though I was in front of a fire. "Okay," I said.

"I just want to tell you one time the way that I feel about you."

"You want to tell me?"

"Yes, and I won't have to tell you again."

I didn't say anything but I nodded.

"I'll tell you this one time," he said, and he shifted from my lap to a sit, facing me. "I won't press you for anything. I promise."

"You're going to tell me?"

"Yes. Please."

"Okay."

"Mel, I'm in love with you."

"Oh God," I said.

"I know," he said. "It's bad."

"Oh no," I said.

"Yes," he said. "I know."

"Stop."

His eyes stayed on mine, unwavering. "You're so beautiful to me, Mel," he said.

"Stop."

"No, Mel. Let me tell you. Let me. Just once." He paused, took a breath. "I look at you and it's too much. I can't take it. I look at you and then when you're not with me I miss you. The way you are with me. You're funny and you make me laugh. You're smart. You're different and I always want to be with you. When I'm not with you, I'm remembering what it's like to be with you. I just sit around and remember you when I'm not with you."

"Oh God," I said.

"I don't want to be with anyone else."

"Jack"—there was disbelief in my voice.

"I don't," he said. "I really don't. I don't want other women. I know what you think. But I don't. I don't think about other women."

"Jack—"

"I think about you."

"Oh no," I said.

"Shut up," he said. "I'm not done."

I said nothing.

"Good," he said. "The other night I had a dream that we were on the ship and I went to your room, but this time you let me hold your hand. That was the dream. Nothing more. I just held your hand on the ship and I felt you holding my hand back. I woke up, and it didn't seem like a dream. It felt real to me. I'm in love with you, Mel. I am."

"Oh no," I said.

"I know," he said. "It's bad. I feel like I'm going to die."

"You're not going to die."

"The idea that you would love me back"—he closed his eyes— "It's too much. It's greedy." He paused, opened his eyes. He stared and I met his stare and he said, "I didn't explain."

"No," I said. "No. You did."

"Really?"

"You explained," I said. "You did."

"Is there a chance?" he said.

He was looking at me as if digging inside me.

"Yes," I said, and then, "No. I mean, yes and no."

"Yes, or do you mean no?"

But he kept his word and didn't press me beyond that.

So there was nothing to do but go back to my room and drink whiskey alone. I took a bath and then lay in my bed with the lights off, watching the stars flickering like a live painting in the frame of the window, feeling the clock-tick of my heartbeat in my temple against the pillow and tucking my flask under my hip between sips.

I thought about Wallace, age sixteen, tall, somewhat gawky, chipped front tooth, open face, solid nose, disheveled red hair, green eyes, ears that stuck out a little, hands that he folded in his lap when he was serious, and feet that were inclined to a duck walk, though he constantly corrected himself, and that habit left him by the time he was twenty. To me, he was good and kind, ambitious, intelligent, curious.

What was I like to him? Youthful and in love, that was what I was like.

I remembered sitting in the swing chair on his parents' porch during that first summer. The big maple leaves scattered at the floor-boards, crunching when we walked over them. Wallace leaning over to smell my hair, and it felt like we were floating, the porch chair creaking in time to our swaying. His lips at my neck and hairline, snapping back to our regular sitting positions with the clap of the porch door, his older sister or his mom come to check on us.

Or driving in his dad's buggy after a year or more together, leaning my head against his shoulder, watching the sky darkening to night. Parking near a neighboring farm. Working on logistics, elbows and knees in cahoots with the angles. Long kisses, quick kisses, and everything in between. Pausing to talk or not talk, it didn't matter. We simply knew that we would be together. The plan: marriage and three children—boy, girl, boy.

Once, he asked me whether I wanted more from life than marriage and kids. Lying in his arms, I said, "It doesn't matter. As long as I'm with you, it doesn't matter."

I believed it, too.

But he didn't.

"I know you," he said.

I didn't answer for a minute. Then I said, "I just want to be with you."

He was quiet, and then he said, "You won't be satisfied. I know you."

I smiled. "Then you know it's true."

He didn't smile and he kept looking at me.

The next day at school he found me between classes and told me, "I meant what I said last night." He made sure I was paying attention. I didn't say anything and then the bell rang and he left for his class. I didn't think any more about it then, but now I think about it. He knew me, he did, and he was anticipating our future.

That next year, my dad had a severe heart attack and died. He didn't like me and I didn't like him, even though I wanted him to love me. The last time I saw him he was reclined in his chair. His eyes fixed on me and he said, "Marry that boy."

"I will," I said, and I shook his hand like we made a business deal, a chill going through my fingers.

At his funeral, I found out that he had married and deserted another woman besides my mother. I knocked against his casket and the sound was hollow. At the reception, I overheard two women in the kitchen mixing lemonade, saying that the stress of my landing on his doorstep when I was nine had been the beginning of his decline.

Two months later, I married Wallace.

I continued to sip whiskey, thinking of Wallace, and not really caring the way that I should that he'd voted against us, and then I slept like a dead person and didn't wake until Farmer banged on my door with breakfast.

The flask was underneath me, and I wedged it under the mattress. She brought me the newspaper, coffee, and two rolls with butter. "No one blames you for his vote," she said, and I told her that I appreciated that.

She was sorry for me, and she let me know it. I expressed my appreciation some more. She pretended not to smell the alcohol. She said not to worry, that she had everything under control. The girls were going shopping, and some reporters and photographers were coming. Did I want to come? I told her that I wanted to rest and she left me to my resting.

I stayed in bed in my Slip Away and Jack came later around dinnertime, with two rolls and a plate of chicken, mashed potatoes, and stringy green beans. He sat down at the chair by the desk, tossing a pack of cigarettes to me.

I took one and patted my nightgown as if looking for matches. He sighed and came forward, leaned in, struck a match.

"Thanks," I said, drawing my head back.

"You're welcome," he replied, and that was the extent of our conversation. He didn't want to know what was on my mind, and I didn't want to know what was on his. Neither of us wanted to say what needed to be said, which was that we had something going on between us, and that he had put it in the open and released it by talking, and that it needed to be discussed more, and how were we going to go forward, with our train leaving in two days, and where would I be living, and did we know what was happening, and what could we do about it? We sat, smoked, stared at each other, and said nothing.

The next morning I bathed and dressed and came back to life, and a reporter interviewed me. He asked me about my husband's vote, and I told him no comment. He told me that our girls beat the American girls in overall scores, which I already knew. Then he asked me more questions about the girls, and I told him that I was happy about our wins, that it felt good to make history. It was a lie. That wasn't what I felt. It was what I wanted to feel. It was what I expected to feel and what people expected of me. It was what I told myself to feel. The answer to his questions should have been a deep and profound silence. But clichés work best for the indefinable and for athletics, and so that was what I offered, and his pencil moved on his pad, because that was what we needed. I gave him the type of answers that his questions wanted, and we both were relieved.

I spent the next hours roaming the streets, drinking strong black coffee in cafés and wondering what the hell was wrong with me.

Chapter Nine
Bell Lap

I went home to Wallace. We treated each other with an awkward deference, our apprehension evident in our long sidelong looks and our silences, and when we did speak, we were polite. I began to sleep late, on the periphery of a bad Slip Away, but I made myself get up, waking to find Wallace up and dressed and staring at me with concern. During the day, he telephoned several times from his office to check on me, our conversations stilted. By the time he got home, I was usually in bed. We made love and it was sad, tender, and familiar.

Often I visited the girls at the Athletic Club and watched them practice when I knew Jack wouldn't be there. But there was a feeling that their glory had ended in Amsterdam, the reality sinking. Something important had happened, something untenable. The feeling, what it meant, had an elusive quality that we couldn't quite grasp. The girls were discovering that life after the Olympics was a letdown. You were expendable. A heroine one day and a nobody the next. There were no college scholarships for women. There were no women coaches. There were no professional jobs. People were not ready for these things, and they still aren't. The girls had competed for the love of sport. But now it was just expensive and hard to justify. If you didn't follow what the press wanted from you like Ginger, they resented you and you hated them and it could only end badly. The papers speculating about a career in Hollywood for the Dream Girl ("I'd rather die a slow death by drinking poison," she responded), and her boyfriends, and what kind of men she desired, and what she ate, how she did her hair, what clothes she preferred, and she sank further into herself each day. The articles were beginning to carry a malicious tone, the latest claiming that money lay at the heart of her relationships with men, describing a pair of black satin pumps with rhinestone buckles, white gloves, three silk scarves, a loose coat of dark gray chinchilla, and a gray velour hat that her latest boyfriend had bought her. Ginger might have gotten a quick thrill from nice things, but I knew that it didn't matter that much to her. She might have been better off had she been more materialistic. But it was a mystery to me what inspired her, and it certainly wasn't things, money, men, or fame.

The other girls didn't attract attention like Ginger. "No one really cares," Flo said, "and there's a bunch of girls ready to replace me." Bonnie was engaged to a quiet businessman, and I couldn't help but wonder if this was her tactic for keeping away from Coach Frank and his family. Danny and Flo were living at the house by the Athletic Club, and Danny was taking secretarial courses. Farmer had this loyalty to give, this eager wisdom and heart, and although her body was breaking, I didn't worry. Hamstring and hip flexor pulls, sciatica, tendinitis, stress fractures, arthritis. At twenty-three she was swallowing half the number of aspirins a day as years she'd been alive, and she was still the one I didn't worry about.

One afternoon, Wallace and I went to a track meet where Ginger was competing. I saw Jack standing there. I wondered if he saw me, but he gave no indication.

Ginger ran toward the high jump, stopped abruptly at the jumping point. She waved her hands in front of her face as if swatting gnats. Then she walked away and the crowd booed and she picked up her pace to a trot. I knew then that the Peerless Four were done with competition, and they were done. Some of them quicker than others, but they were done.

Driving home, Wallace said, "Why do women want to be men?"

"Careful."

He wouldn't look at me. "No," he said, "you be careful."

At the house, I brooded over what he'd said, wondering: does he want me to leave him? He was pretending not to know me or respect me, denying my core.

By the next day, the incident didn't seem as potent. I loved him and love was enough. But I couldn't help but worry that what was important to me was what he wouldn't acknowledge. What most defined me was what he didn't want to believe. At times I would watch him when he wasn't looking, and a fear would come over me that our marriage was an excuse for my giving up.

Sometimes Wallace was responsive. Affectionate and tender, gaining energy as mine was exhausted, like a teeter-totter. In the middle of dinner, he might lean forward across the table and kiss me. His hand would reach to hold mine.

Yet at other times I would catch him looking at me as if trying to gain dominion by the force of his concentration. Instead of looking away, he would continue to stare. I was amazed at the breadth of license he took in these examinations, as if controlling me through strength of will. I would feel a sickening depletion mixed with shame, wondering if it were true. Did he control me?

"I love you," he said.

"I know."

"I mean it."

"I love you, too."

I wondered, what if I hadn't married Wallace? What if I'd never met him? Would it have all happened with another man? Would I belong to that other man? When I watched him one morning parting and combing his hair, I felt that I could not love him when he tried to control me.

Alone in the house, I read books in Wallace's study and practiced holding his guns before the mirror. I had no desire to return to my job. Jack said that I could come back anytime, but all that seemed unattainable now. I was broody, confused. While I was reading, my vision blurred. I napped often, twitched and jerked in my sleep. I dreamt my hair and teeth were falling out, my limbs dissolving. At times I wondered if I was crazy.

When Wallace came home, I buried my face in him, and a sense of calmness and comfort came over me. When we made love, there was a reprieve. After, I lay with him with a sense of indulgence. I caressed him in admiration. His substantial body showed signs of age and decline and so did mine. Right above his rump there was a triangle of soft tufty hair that I adored. We were accustomed to each other, our sexual regimen comfortable. I wondered if he was bored by our familiarity, but he continued to reach for me.

The weeks passed, and then Wallace started leaving for work early and coming home late. I woke after he left and ate my breakfast looking out the kitchen window, watching for hummingbirds at a feeder that hung in our tree.

One day at the Athletic Club I walked over to find Jack sitting at the stands of the basketball court. He hadn't shaved and he needed a haircut.

"Where've you been?" he asked and I didn't answer. He said that his Dream Girl franchise was no longer in play, now that Ginger had eloped with a businessman.

"Is it true?"

He shrugged. "Probably."

We stared at each other, thinking about Ginger. I had an image of her as an old woman with her ukulele and rag doll, tossing her gold medals in the trash, hiding from people, bitter and alone. But maybe it wouldn't be that awful.

"They just wanted to win," he said. "They didn't know what it meant."

"We didn't know, either."

"That's true," he said. "We didn't."

The next morning, I ate toast with butter and two poached eggs and then headed to the Athletic Club again. It was a warm day, warmer than usual. The sky looked like the blue had been bleached a little, and there were no clouds except at the mountains. There weren't many people at the club because of the good weather, and no Jack.

At the indoor pool, I watched some girls tossing a ball, splashing and yelling, and they sensed me, one of them holding the ball for a second, sending me a stare. She wore a swimming cap that made her look bald, all eyes and mouth and stare, but it was over soon and she turned from me and threw the ball, and they were at it again. Water splashed on my dress, splotching the material a dark blue near my hip.

I sat midway at the bleachers of the empty basketball court. I had my notebook and a novel, and I read and wrote and switched back again, pausing to smoke a cigarette. When I heard voices, I looked up to see a boy and a girl approaching the court, dribbling a basketball between them.

The boy set the ball down and they stretched: touching their toes, swinging their hips, reaching their arms up and leaning from side to side. He was tall with a long chest and big arms and no extra weight to show. His dark hair was cut close, and there was a bit of chest hair springing from the V of his shirt. He wore vivid blue shorts, the color like the blue inside a flame. She was also tall, about to his shoulders, with bobbed brown hair and straight-cut bangs, and when she moved, her hair flicked about. She wore white shoes and bloomers and her legs were brown and muscular. They were young, probably in their late teens or early twenties.

They began playing and I pretended to read but I watched. I could tell by their skills that they meant business. But then the boy seemed to be letting her win. After some time, he got serious because she was moving him around the court and making him sweat. I couldn't tell if they were keeping score, but they seemed to have their own system. He got the ball from her and she sprung after him, slapping at the ball to steal it back. Their shoes squeaked. Elbows and knees butted against each other. She was pretty and quick and she reminded me of Ginger.

As I watched I yearned to be on the court with them. I'm the kind of spectator who longs to participate. But then I remembered that my body and reflexes weren't young and, for an overpowering second, that my life was that much closer to death. A little dot in a trajectory beginning at birth, nearer now to the end. It seemed to me then that the finish line at the end of a life was similar to the finish line at the end of a race, both giving off a magnetic, inevitable force.

The girl got the ball from the boy and he was surprised. She dribbled, took a shot. The ball spun at the rim, then dropped through the hoop. "Yes," she said, "my game," and I couldn't tell what he was thinking, his back turned to me.

There was a twinge in my stomach and I wanted to warn her, "There's going to be another game, and another, and another. It never ends, and you'll end up losing. You'll lose until you can't win anymore." I wanted to tell her that we cling to the clichés and fantasies of our meager selves. We play sports and buck against our insignificance. We talk, rant, swear, and debate with each other and to ourselves, because no matter what, life ends with the ultimate loss.

But it was useless for me to impart my opinions because she would have to find out for herself the terrible beauty of losing. Stupefying, inevitable, necessary. Connected to the great empty spaces of death. Why should this be disappointing? Isn't the emptiness at its essence similar to the blank whistle of nothing that courses through an athlete's mind when she makes her best shot, jump, or throw?

The girl might listen politely and nod her head, but she was young and wouldn't believe me. She looked so youthful and open that for a second I didn't believe me either. I didn't want to believe me. But I had Ginger, Flo, Farmer, and Bonnie to remind me, the Peerless Four to thank for my knowledge.

I left before their second game ended so that I didn't see who won, but I heard the boy say, "Good shot," and she said, "You're not trying," and he laughed. I wanted to kick him for feeding her the ball, because it was better to lose going all out than to win from fakery. I heard him laugh again, and I knew that he wouldn't play his best. He wouldn't let her plunge into loss.

That way, no matter how good or bad she was, she wouldn't be his equal. It didn't matter if she won. If she wasn't allowed to lose by the same rules, if she didn't question the equation that men are always stronger, faster, smarter, and if she merely accepted her place as revolving around this assumption, then her life wouldn't be hers because it would belong to him.

That night, I sat in bed and stared at Wallace sleeping, trying not to stare too hard and wake him. Maneuvering my body beside him, I stroked his hair, arms, and back. I felt protective and sad. Then I must have fallen asleep because he was shaking me awake.

I turned on the bedside lamp and he was looking at me in alarm.

"What happened?" I asked.

"I want you to leave," he said. There was fear in his eyes. "Just go." He said that I acted like a trapped animal. Then he lowered his head and was looking at his hands. He said in a low voice, "It's better when you're not here."

I said that I agreed. I would stay at the house near the Athletic Club with Danny and Flo.

We didn't talk much after that. He looked up and said, "I love you," and I told him that I loved him, too. We sat and held hands but we didn't disturb our equilibrium by opening a conversation to problems with no solutions. There was no way to sleep, so I made pancakes and we ate in silence and watched for the sun through the kitchen window. Later he drove me to the house, my three suitcases rattling in the backseat. It had rained sometime during the night, and in the glimmering sunlight everything had a light, washed, fervent look, as if just realizing what it meant to be a tree, house, roof, sky.

Chapter Ten

Flight Phase

—∘—

March 19, 1935
My dearest Mel,

Can it really be over a year since we've corresponded and over four since we've been in each other's company? I take pen in hand to write to you, as you have been heavy on my heart and mind.

The weeks and months spin past me and then a year has gone, and another, and another. I must admit that I did not know that period of time at the Olympics was to be the peak of my athletic life. It passed without my reflection on its ending. I still thought my skills would improve.

My greatest achievement has come and gone, and I didn't realize it until it was long gone. I've been rubbed, patted, squeezed, and kneaded, and still my muscles and joints resist.

All of a sudden, it seemed like my strength got zapped out of me. I had no more strength to compete. I finished last in a race, and I'd never

finished last before. I got home that night, and
my legs ached like somebody had taken a knife
to them. I got in the tub and soaked and said to
myself, It's okay. It's over. It's okay. It's over. I'd
never had that feeling before. That night it suddenly dawned on me that I had gone as far as I was
ever going to go. I knew that I couldn't go all out
anymore, and when you know that, you can't go
on competing.

As you know, I had eight months in bed in surrender to my physical maladies. I am reconciled to
this life of aches and pains. Don't feel bad for me!
I find in it consolation and hope. There is pleasure
for me in strength and fortitude. To sweat in agony
and suffer and shed tears, and then to persevere
and know that I can persevere. The satisfaction is
greater, the peace, after the struggle. My greatest
moments of well-being have come after pain.

With improvement and resolve, I have cobbled
together a very good life at the *Toronto Daily Star*,
and now I am their top reporter and editor for
women's sports. Thank you again for your advice
and suggestions. I didn't mention your name, but
you underestimate your reputation.

I have been able, as you suggested, to get what I
want by squeezing and hiding my words inside the
words the paper demands from me, and thus have
agency within their usual patterns. A reader must
read close to find my words, but mine are there
and that makes it worthwhile. I never did enjoy
being a spectator. I was the type of athlete who

went crazy watching, because I needed to be out there competing, but it's different now that I write about it.

You'll be interested to know that Bonnie has taken up golf and curling and is quite good. I wrote a brief article about her. Two children. Hung up her track shoes for the domestic, she says. Doesn't want to compete much anymore. Says she can't psyche herself up again. She's not bitter. "If I'd won that gold in my event," she said, "I probably wouldn't be as happy as I am today. I wouldn't have had to search things out." She makes a point to stay out of the spotlight, but she is doing well.

I saw Flo at a party and met her husband. She didn't invite me to her wedding and so it was a bit awkward. I'm sure you already know that she is married. He's a Bell Telephone district manager and seems devoted to her. She dropped out of high school but she told me that she graduated from the Margaret Eaton School of Physical Education. She never did like school. We talked briefly about the Games. "I was strong enough to win my heat," she said, "but I floundered in the finals."

I told her that despite her injury, she had run her fastest time ever. She had to be proud of that. "You ran faster," I said, "then you'd ever run before. That's not losing. Some of the girls just happened to run faster than you on that day." She said, "I didn't do what I wanted to do," and her husband said, "You were just too young." She lives with regret and disappointment, but I hope in time she might realize the significance of her achievements.

Strangely, the following afternoon I saw Coach Sacks after a track meet. He was limping and whispering to himself, probably curses, headed for his car. His girls hadn't placed and he was upset. At first I was going to leave him alone, but I caught up with him and we talked. He asked me, "It's true, isn't it?" I didn't understand until he continued, "She got married," and then I realized that he was talking about Flo. I guess he wasn't invited to the wedding either. I told him that it was a fact. We looked at each other for a long time and said nothing, and then he said that he had to leave.

By the way, I heard about Wallace's remarriage to the widow Gracie Majors, and his raising of her three children. They're all under five years of age? He certainly has his hands full. I assume that you are good with everything.

Women love men and live in a world of men who make the rules. Women might not agree, but they still love the men who made and make and enforce these rules. I've always believed this to be your test. Loving men without succumbing, not missing out on loving men. Discerning your own path. Men and women are joined and glued to each other and cannot be detached without the tearing of skin and organ, and that is painful. Being vigilant and loving, and that's not easy and has never been my challenge.

I know that you know this but I have never told you. I don't love men but I have to live with them and inside their rules. I have to find my own path. It can feel like trying to destroy the fog by flinging a stick of dynamite into it. It doesn't work. It's loud and bright and causes a scene but the fog is still there. It can feel like it's all around and everywhere and inside me, influential and ingenious. It can overwhelm me. But then I remember that I do not wish to have everything that I wish. I like to have everything happen as it happens, and then my life is good.

I often remember finding you running near the Athletic Club. How you tried to jump from my sight! Even thinking about it now brings a grin to my face. It reminds me of all that is unique, what can't be categorized, and what is mysterious and continually surprises me. And then I remember that I don't want to have everything that I wish, that I like to be surprised.

Please give Jack my best. I hope you are enjoying Montana and that Jack is resting and recovering satisfactorily. Is he able to live without his cigarettes? A stroke is a serious matter, but three strokes! I don't care if they're "mild." Three strokes! I must admit, I can't imagine him living a clean life. Retired! In fact, tug his ear, smack his backside, and kiss him full on the mouth, then tell him that's from Farmer.

This morning I woke and knew I could wait no longer. I had to write to you. Last month we were called into a meeting and told that we were not to report the news. Can you imagine? Reporters told not to report. The decision comes from high up and is final. But I have lived with the information and find that you are the one person I know who will understand as I do.

I must ask for your discretion. My job depends on it. I know that I can count on you and trust you, but I must ask.

Hugh Williams took his life with a self-inflicted gunshot wound to his heart. He shot his heart out, Mel. No suicide note, but he used that gun that they gave him as a prize for his Olympic victories—remember that big silver gun the mayor presented to him at that other ceremony after that small one?—which to me IS his note.

Last year he donated his golds to the Sports Hall of Fame. Remember the uproar when they were stolen? That was the last time I spoke to him. The paper sent me. Everyone wanted to know if his golds would be replaced. They sent me because I was at the Olympics with him. So they sent a woman reporter, which they never would've done. Would he demand that his golds be replaced? I questioned him and he didn't care. That was his exact quote: "I don't care," and he shrugged. "So what if I was once the world's greatest runner," he said. "When I go to the store for milk, the clerk still wants his money." He was an insurance agent. Skinny and sad-looking with glasses. He suffered from arthritis like me, lived with his mom, and he told me that he did it all for her and for his coach and that he didn't like to run. "I was just a kid," he said. "I was bewildered. Oh, I was so glad to get out of it." That was the last time we spoke.

Isn't it so strange? The government makes them heroes, and they don't care. They don't care! So we're not supposed to report it because of our national pride? It makes me look back on the parades and the ceremonies and all those speeches, and even the Olympics. It seems to me that people like to hold athletes up and make them heroes because it makes people feel important. They want to have a feeling of consequence, to advance their politics and national interests, and to simply not think about life, so they make them heroes.

The real Games are about human performance, about real people excelling at sport under great pressure and a global spotlight. Of course there's the nationalism, politics, and discrimination, but the Olympics changed me, and not because I won gold. My knowledge and appreciation of the world and various cultures has enriched my life. It changed my politics. It changed everything. There's a humanity that we all have in common, no matter our differences and nationalities. We have a physical, intellectual, emotional, and spiritual connection through our humanity, and I learned this.

But for Hugh and Ginger, the press turned them into human billboards, and no wonder they both turned their backs. Like Dr. Frankensteins, the press possessed, created, invented, and cast them.

Ginger's fate was a bit different because she was a female beauty first, with athlete a close second.

Now I'm not supposed to report any of it. I'm supposed to arrange, regulate, and fix the truth to suit the public's idolatry.

Do great athletes ever die satisfied, Mel? How do they live with decline? These questions plague me. But then I'm proof that it is possible. I live well. I have my dog and my house and we are happy. It is enough for me to watch my dog dreaming with her legs twitching and see and know that she has an inner world just like mine. I love her and we have our relationship and that is good. It is enough.

I've been doing so much thinking and remembering about us—about the Peerless Four and what it all means. Do sports have meaning and mystery like life? We create meaning and it's like Sisyphus and his rock going up the hill and then the rock rolling down again. Always another game, another chance. No one stays a winner eternally.

I think about girls and history and progress. I meet these girl athletes now, and they don't seem to want to acknowledge the women who made strides before them, so that they could have it better. Why do women betray that? Why pretend it's not connected to their lives? Is it because it's easier not to acknowledge and accept?

I decided to write an article but the paper nixed it right away when they saw what I was up to. I'd already gone to Grass Valley, California, by then, made a trip to interview Ginger. I wanted to see for myself if the reports were true. There was a rumor that she sicced her dog on the last reporter who tried to talk to her. Her divorce came through. She was married to two at one time. Did you know that? She divorced both of them, and then one more. Now she is alone, just like she wanted.

Danny's married and living in Vancouver. She's doing okay. She doesn't want to talk about Ginger, though. I tried. "I'm through," she said. "I have my own life now."

I went to Grass Valley and found Ginger. Her house sits back from the others on a residential street, accessible only by a dirt path and sheltered behind these large, overlapping trees. She doesn't own a telephone, so I couldn't call to let her know that I was coming. Even before I made it up the front porch steps, she was peering at me through her living room curtains. It was an overcast afternoon reminding me of Amsterdam, and it seemed that it would start raining (though it never did).

She's the town recluse, known to be cold and aloof, and when I asked around about her at city hall beforehand, a woman told me that she'd seen Ginger only once, pushing a shopping cart at the grocery store (apparently Ginger pays a boy to deliver her groceries each week) and wearing a baseball hat. The woman said that when Ginger stopped in front of the canned soups, she passed her hand across her throat, and that for some reason this gesture seemed sad and elegant. That's what the woman told me. Sad and elegant. That's the most I got out of anyone.

Ginger stared right at me from between those curtains when I walked up her front porch. Her face looked open, Mel—as open as I'd ever seen it. That's the only way I can describe it. For a second she was like a kid. But when I nodded, her face tightened, and then those curtains closed around her. I knocked but she wouldn't come to the door. I knocked again. "It's just me," I said. "I know you saw me. I'm not leaving. I'll just stay here."

A long time passed, and then she finally opened the door a crack from its chain lock. There was this big black Doberman growling at me with pink gums, and she shushed him and called him Dog, so I guess his name is Dog. "Sit, Dog," she said. "Stay, Dog." The house was dark but it didn't look dirty, and I could see a radio and a couch and the kitchen table.

We stood in a sort of stunned adjustment, not talking. I wondered if she knew about Hugh but I wasn't going to be the one to tell her. She wore these blue socks bunched around her ankles, and the buttons on her robe gaped at her bust. Her hair was pulled from her face by a tortoiseshell headband and she was trying to be unattractive but it wasn't working. She's still so pretty, Mel. She can't shake her beauty.

"Leave me alone," she finally said.

I didn't know what to say.

"I know about Hugh," she said, and she looked right at me. She looked at me until I looked away. We stood with me not facing her for a while, and then she shushed Dog again because he'd begun whimpering.

"What do you want?" she asked.

"I don't know," I said, and I didn't know. I thought I knew but I didn't. I suppose I wanted to know that she would be okay, and that she wouldn't shoot herself in the heart like her friend. But I didn't know at the time, and even if I did, I wouldn't have known how to tell her.

"I'm sorry," I said, "really sorry, that you feel like you have to hide."

"A person can disappear," she said. "With effort and money, a person can disappear. Even the Dream Girl," and her face went down. She was sorry about it all, and that was what she was telling me. So I left her.

What I feared at that very instant as I walked down her porch steps is what I still fear: that I somehow contributed to her demise. That I had made her into the Dream Girl like the others.

She called out: "Thank you, Farmer." Instead of turning to face her, I raised my hand in the air.

This morning it started to rain, and after some time, the rain turned to ice and then to snow. I knew that I would write you and let you know what is on my heart and mind because you are on my heart and mind, connected to everything that I write. Please write me back when you can.

Truly yours,
Muriel

I read Farmer's letter over and over for days, and I did tug Jack's ear, slap his backside, kiss him full on the mouth, and tell him, That's from Farmer. I shared the letter with him and he kept silent about its contents. The only thing he did say was that I would wear out the paper with all my readings. He moved slowly, lumbering from room to room. His face sagged on the left side. Often he lay on his back on the floor, his arms up and stretched over his head as if in surrender—palms open—and his feet and legs extended on the wall. Like an L. Eyes squinted shut and breathing deeply. This position was the most comfortable, he told me. Otherwise he was the same. He smoked cigarettes behind the barn and took hits from his flask. I found the butts and smelled the nicotine and whiskey but pretended not to know. But we drank and smoked less and did so without each other's company.

It took me a week to decide what to write back to Farmer. I ran in the late afternoons, when the sun was low. I could see the shining river with the ducks and birds gathered there and, on clear days, the hazy snow-peaked mountains toward Canada, blue-tinted and darkening in the vanishing light. When I finished, the waxing moon was visible, fuller each time. I thought about how to respond to Farmer. I ran and ran and ran, on through the fields and into the woods, up and down went my legs, in and out went my arms, my breath and feet corresponding. I crossed creeks and listened, thinking about nothing but how to respond. I thought about how women have struggled so long and resolute, and how our accomplishments carry a resonance of sacrifice, struggle, and elusive victory gained over incredible odds. How the doctors told me that I wouldn't have babies, and that my uterus would fall out. I don't have children, but it's not because I run. I don't know why I couldn't.

The sky was as big as Canada, with puffy clouds, and the river a chill slate gray. Tall trees lined the bank. Sometimes the faces of Wallace's children and his wife would flash through me, for he'd sent a photograph. He was still a part of me and now they were, too, and their faces would flash through me, and my skin would prickle with sorrow and joy. My eyes would go wet, and then their faces would be gone. I'd see Danny and Ginger, Flo and Bonnie, and Farmer. They were me and I was them and then I would go to a deeper place that I can't explain. I only know that what I felt was bigger than me. Honest and real and the fact of it would be there no matter what I felt at other times or went through, and no matter what anybody else told me or tried to tell me, because it was mine and belonged inside me. But it was also connected to something bigger and beyond me and outside me.

I understood this best that week when my feet pulled me forward on the ground. I ended up more within myself, and more outside myself. I passed a decomposing bird on my path, its feathers and bones ground into the earth a little more each time, and I would think, Things are here and then they're over, and that's enough, all the while tasting the vast spread of time's abyss, and the universe and infinity, and my small life, and then one afternoon the bird was earth.

Then came the stopping. The physical relief of being done. Walking and returning. Smelling the piney metallic air. Coming home to Jack. His openness helped me open up, and drew me out, and when all is said and done, he told me once, it's all about the love. Even when it's not about the love it's about the love. It's just the love. We're pieced together from each other and we're shapeless yet each of us touches the other. We play our games, and in the end there are winners and losers and losers and winners, and you try your best just the same. Each bit, each moment, plays its own game, and slow, slow, slowly—and sometimes quickly—things change, and sometimes you're part of that change.

Regardless, I need to hold on to my inner self—my inner freedom—for this is my most valuable substance. But I know very little, my knowledge puny when reflected against this astounding world.

Instead of trying to explain all of this to Farmer, I wrote on the backside of a postcard of a moose: *I miss and love you. I will visit soon. Yours always, Mel.*

I never did worry about Farmer. She was ahead of me and didn't need my elucidation.

I mailed my postcard. Then I went for a run.

Before the Peerless Four[*]

776 BC—The first Olympics are held in ancient Greece without women, so women compete every four years in their own Games of Hera, in honor of the Greek goddess who ruled over women and the earth.

396 BC—Kyniska, a Spartan princess, wins an Olympic chariot race but is barred from collecting her prize in person.

1406—Dame Julian Berners of Great Britain writes "Treatise of Fishing with an Angle," the first known essay on sportfishing, describing how to make a rod and flies, when to fish, and the many kinds of fishing.

1784—Elizabeth Thible of Lyons, France, is the first woman to soar in a hot-air balloon.

1798—France's Jeanne Labrosse makes a solo balloon flight.

---

[*] This is just a small sampling.

1805—Madeleine Sophie Aramant Blanchard solos in the first of sixty-seven gas-powered balloon flights. She made her living as a balloonist, was appointed official Aeronaut of the Empire by Napoleon, and toured Europe. She fell to her death in an aerial fireworks display in 1819.

1805—Englishwoman Alicia Meynell, riding as Mrs. Thornton, defeats a leading male jockey.

1811—On January 9, the first known women's golf tournament is held at Musselburgh Golf Club, Scotland, among the town fishwives.

1819—Mademoiselle Adophe is the first woman tightrope performer in New York City.

1825—Madame Johnson takes off in a hot-air balloon in New York, landing in a New Jersey swamp.

1850—Amelia Jenks Bloomers begins publicizing a new style of women's dress, first introduced by Fanny Kemble, a British-born actress—loose-fitting pants worn under a skirt. Women's rights leaders such as Elizabeth Cady Stanton and Susan B. Anthony adopt the new style.

1856—*Physiology and Calisthenics for Schools and Families*, by Catherine Beecher, is published; it is the first fitness manual for women.

1858—Wearing bloomers, Julia Archibald Holmes climbs Pikes Peak in Colorado.

1867—The Dolly Vardens, a black women's professional baseball team from Philadelphia, is formed.

1871—Carrie A. Moore demonstrates a variety of roller-skating movements at the Occidental Rink in San Francisco. Later in the same day, she exhibits her skill on a velocipede.

1873—Ten young women compete in a mile-long swimming contest in the Harlem River. Delilah Goboess wins the prize, a silk dress worth $175.

1874—Mary Ewing Outerbridge of Staten Island introduces tennis to the United States. She purchases tennis equipment in Bermuda, has difficulty getting it through customs, and uses it to set up the first U.S. tennis court at the Staten Island Cricket and Baseball Club.

1875—Lizzie Ihling, the niece of famed American balloonist John Wise, makes a solo flight. The skin of the bag rips, sending the balloon falling to earth. Lizzie is not injured.

1875—The Blondes and the Brunettes play their first match in Springfield, Illinois. Newspapers herald the event as the "first game of baseball ever played in public for gate money between feminine ball-tossers."

1875—English teenager Agnes Beckwith swims a long-distance six miles in the Thames River.

1876—Mary Marshal, twenty-six, shocks spectators by beating Peter Van Ness in the best-of-three walking matches (called Pedestrians) in New York City.

1876—Maria Speltarini crosses Niagara Falls on a tightrope, wearing thirty-eight-pound weights on each ankle.

1876—Nell Saunders defeats Rose Harland in the first U.S. women's boxing match, winning a silver butter dish.

1878—Woman pedestrian Ada Anderson walks around the inside of New York's Mozart Hall three thousand times in one month, accruing 750 miles total during this time and inspiring a series of "lady walker" matches.

1880—Distance swimmer Agnes Beckwith treads water for thirty hours in the whale tank of the Royal Aquarium of Westminster to equal a previous mark set by Mathew Webb.

1881—Edith Johnson of England sets the world's endurance indoor swimming record at thirty-one hours. The record holds until 1928.

1884—Women's singles tennis competition is added to Wimbledon. Maud Watson wins.

1885—The Association of Collegiate Alumnae publishes a study concluding that "it is sufficient to say that female graduates . . . do not seem to show . . . any marked difference in general health for the average health . . . of women engaged in other kinds of work, or in fact, of women generally," refuting the widely held belief that college study impairs a woman's physical health and ability to bear children.

1885—Annie Oakley is the sharpshooting star of Buffalo Bill's Wild West show. She can hit a moving target while riding a galloping horse, hit a dime in midair, and regularly shoots a cigarette from her husband's lips.

1886—Mary Hawley Myers sets a world altitude record in a hot-air balloon, soaring four miles above Franklin, Pennsylvania, without benefit of oxygen equipment. Between 1800 and 1890, she completes more balloon ascents than any other living person.

1887—Rose Coghlin competes in a mixed trapshooting match held at Philadelphia Gun Club. She and two men tie, each scoring seven.

1888—Berta Benz becomes the first woman to drive on a sixty-mile cross-country trip in Germany in a "motor-wagon" (a three-horsepower car with solid rubber tires). Only her teenage sons accompany her.

1889—Isobel Stanley is one of the first hockey players in Canada. Her Government House team plays the Rideau Ladies in what may be the first women's hockey game in Ottawa.

1890s—More than a million American women own and ride bicycles during this decade. For the first time in American history, an athletic activity for women becomes widely popular, with the development of the modern-style "safety bicycle." The bike has two equal-sized wheels, coaster brakes, and pneumatic tires creating a comfortable, faster, and safer ride. A side effect is more commonsense dressing for women. Susan B. Anthony says, "The bicycle has done more for the emancipation of women than anything else in the world."

1890s—The Bloomer Girls baseball era lasts from the 1890s until 1934. Hundreds of teams—All Star Ranger Girls, Philadelphia Bobbies, New York Bloomer Girls, Baltimore Black Socks Colored Girls—offer employment, travel, and adventure for young women who can hit, field, slide, or catch.

1890—As a reporter for the *New York World*, Nellie Bly (Elizabeth Cochran Seaman) becomes the first woman to travel around the world alone in 72 days, completing the fastest circumnavigation of the globe at that time, for anyone, male or female.

1890—Fay Fuller climbs 14,410-foot Mount Rainier in Washington.

1891—Zoe Gayton arrives in Castleton, New York, after walking cross-country in 213 days, averaging eighteen miles per day and winning a two-thousand-dollar wager.

1891—Mary French Sheldon mounts her first expedition to East Africa. Her travel accounts break scientific and anthropological territory by focusing on women and children. She is one of only twenty-two women invited to join the Royal Geographic Society in 1892. The invitation is withdrawn after contentious debate about women's presence within the society. She eventually makes four trips around the world.

1892—The journal *Physical Education* (published by the YMCA) devotes an issue to women, claiming that women need physical strength and endurance and dismissing the popular idea that women are too weak to exercise.

1892—While at the University of Nebraska, Louise Pound helps organize a girls' military company and she sets a record at rifle practice. She is the first woman named to the Lincoln Journal Sports Hall of Fame. She participates in tennis, golf, cycling, and ice skating, and coaches girls' basketball. She makes pioneering contributions to American philology and folklore.

1892—Hessie Donahue dons a loose blouse, bloomers, and boxing gloves to spar a few rounds as part of a vaudeville act and knocks out legendary heavyweight champion John L. Sullivan for over a minute after he accidentally lands a real blow on her.

1893—Sixteen-year-old Tessie Reynolds of Brighton rides her bicycle to London and back, a distance of 120 miles, in 8½ hours. She wears the shocking "rationale" dress—a long jacket over knickers, which outrages some observers as much as her feat does.

1893—Inspired after climbing to the top of Pikes Peak, Katherine Lee Bates composes "America, the Beautiful."

1894—College girls at McGill University in Montreal begin weekly ice hockey games at an indoor rink with three male "guards" at the door.

1894—Annie "Londonderry" Kopchovsky sets out to become the first woman to bicycle around the world, a journey that lasts fifteen months and earns her five thousand dollars.

1895—Annie Smith Peck is the first woman to reach the peak of the Matterhorn. She climbs in a pair of knickerbockers, causing a sensation with the press.

1895—The first organized athletics meeting is generally recognized as the "Field Day" at Vassar College. A group of "nimble, supple, and vivacious girls" engages in running and jumping despite bad weather.

1896—The first women's intercollegiate basketball championship is played between Stanford and the University of California, Berkeley. Stanford wins, 2 to 1, on April 4 before a crowd of seven hundred women.

1896—At the first modern Olympics in Athens, a woman, Melpomene, barred from the official race, runs the same course as the men's, finishing in four hours, thirty minutes. Baron Pierre de Coubertin says, "It is indecent that the spectators should be exposed to the risk of seeing the body of a woman being smashed before their eyes. Besides, no matter how toughened a sportswoman may be, her organism is not cut out to sustain certain shocks."

1897—Lena Jordan becomes the first person to successfully execute the triple somersault on the flying trapeze. The first man doesn't do so until 1909.

1898—Lizzie Arlington becomes the first woman to sign a professional baseball contract, appearing in her first professional game pitching for the Philadelphia Reserves.

1900-1920—Physical education instructors strongly oppose competition among women, fearing it will make them less feminine.

1900—The first nineteen women to compete in the modern Olympic Games in Paris play in three sports: tennis, golf, and croquet.

1901—Annie Taylor, forty-three, becomes the first person to go over Niagara Falls in a custom-built barrel and lives, even though she can't swim. On being retrieved, she says, "Nobody ever ought to do that again."

1901—Ambidextrous Mary Karlus, sixteen, performs a series of amazing billiard shots in New York City. Male experts try and fail to duplicate.

1903—Eleanor Roosevelt enrolls in the Junior League of New York, where she teaches calisthenics and dancing to immigrants.

1903—A women's curling team from Quebec City defeats a men's curling team from the Royal Caledonia in Scotland.

1903—Cuban-born Aida de Acosta pilots a dirigible over Paris, just months before the Wright brothers fly at Kitty Hawk, North Carolina.

1904—Amanda Clement, sixteen, becomes the first female umpire to officiate a men's baseball game in Iowa for pay.

1904—Bertha Kapernick is the first woman to give bronco riding exhibitions at the Cheyenne Frontier Days rodeo.

1906—Lula Olive Gill is the first woman jockey to win a horse race in California.

1906—Ada Evans Dean rides her horse to victory twice in Liberty, New York, after learning that her jockey is ill. She has never ridden in a horse race before.

1907—Annette Kellerman is the first underwater ballerina at the New York Hippodrome. The Australian native attracts attention when she appears at Boston's Revere beach in a one-piece bathing suit.

1908—In England, Muriel Matters, a suffragist and balloonist, flies over the British House of Parliament, dropping hundreds of flyers urging "votes for women."

1909—Annie Smith Peck, fifty-seven, becomes the first person to climb 21,000-foot Mount Huascaran, the highest peak in Peru. Her last climb is Mount Madison, New Hampshire, at age eighty-two.

1910—Clelia Duel Mosher, a physician, debunks several popular myths of female health, including one claiming that women breathe differently than men and are thus unfit for strenuous exercise.

1910—Baroness Raymonde de Laroche passes her qualifying tests to become the first woman in the world to be issued a pilot's license.

1910—Australia's Annette Kellerman is arrested for swimming in Boston Harbor in an "indecent" one-piece swimsuit, exposing her legs.

1911—Harriet Quimby makes her professional aviator debut with a moonlit flight over Staten Island before a crowd of twenty thousand spectators to become the first woman to make a night flight.

1911—At sixty-one, Annie Smith Peck plants a "Votes for Women" banner on top of Mount Coropuna in Peru when she becomes the first woman to climb it.

1911—Helene Britton becomes the first woman owner of a major league team, the St. Louis Cardinals, from 1911 to 1917.

1912—Harriet Quimby is the first woman to pilot an airplane across the English Channel. For most of the flight, she flies through fog and depends on her compass.

1912—Swimming and diving debut at the Stockholm Olympic Games, with fifty-seven women from eleven nations competing.

1913—American Alys McKey Bryant becomes the first woman to fly a plane in Canada. She performs an exhibition flight for Prince Albert, Duke of York. She learns to fly after winning a job to perform in flight demonstrations. She marries John Bryant, one of the pilots who hires her, and ends her flying career after his death.

1914—Georgia "Tiny" Broadwick, demonstrating air-jumping techniques to the U.S. Army in San Diego, pulls her release manually, becoming the first person to make an intentional free-fall parachute jump from an airplane.

1914—The American Olympic Committee formally opposes women's athletic competition in the Olympics. The only exception is floor exercises, where women are required to wear long skirts.

1915—The British government appoints Gertrude Bell as diplomat in Baghdad because of her knowledge of the territory. She is the first European woman to travel in remote parts of the Middle East. She travels, often alone, and writes about her journeys.

1916—Sisters Adeline and Augusta Van Buren become the first women to ride motorcycles across the country. They also are the first women to conquer the 14,100-foot summit of Pikes Peak on motorcycles.

1916—Ruth Law flies nonstop from Chicago to Hornell, New York, setting the American nonstop cross-country record for both men and women. She has installed auxiliary gas tanks, upping her fuel capacity from eight to fifty-three gallons, and adds a rubber gas line to her open "pusher" type Curtiss plane.

1917—Charlotte "Eppie" Epstein, a court reporter, rents one of New York City's only chlorinated pools (in the basement of Brooklyn's Hotel Terrain) and founds the Women's Swimming Association of New York, dedicated to competitive training for women.

1917—Lucy Diggs Slowe wins the singles title at the first American Tennis Association national tournament, becoming the first female African American national champion in any sport.

1918—Eleonora Sears (a great-great-granddaughter of Thomas Jefferson) takes up squash, after excelling at polo (she rides astride on the horse, shocking conventions of the day), baseball, golf, field, hockey, auto racing, swimming, tennis, yachting, and speedboat racing. She accumulates 240 trophies during her athletic career. Demonstrating that women can play men's games, she is a prime role model for women in sports.

1918—Lillian Leitzel, thirty-six, a ninety-pound acrobat and aerialist with Ringling Bros. and Barnum & Bailey Circus, beats the 1878 world's record of twelve one-armed chin-ups. She performs twenty-seven such chin-ups with her right arm; switching to her left, she did nineteen more.

1920s—The fashions of the time put a new emphasis on athletic bodies and narrow the gap between health and glamour. Advertisers like Grape Nuts say, "Grandmothers went bathing—girls like Molly go in to swim."

1920—Theresa Weld Blanchard wins the first U.S. medal in the Winter Olympics, a bronze for figure skating. She is scolded for putting a jump into her program.

1920—The Dick, Kerr's Ladies professional soccer team tours the United States, outscoring their male opponents.

1920—At the Summer Olympics, France's Suzanne Lenglen abandons the customary tennis garb for a short, pleated skirt, sleeveless silk blouse, and matching sweater. She wins two golds and a bronze, becoming the first female celebrity athlete.

1921—Bessie Coleman becomes the first black licensed pilot in the world.

1921—Adrienne Bolland becomes the first woman to fly over the Andes, taking off from Mendoza, Argentina, and landing ten hours later in Santiago de Chile. She flies at an altitude of 14,750 feet in bitter cold, avoiding mountain peaks that are higher than the altitude her plane can fly.

1921—Phoebe Fairgrave becomes the first woman to do a double parachute jump, cutting away her first parachute and opening a second. In the 1930s, she organizes a group of women fliers to barnstorm the country urging communities to paint the name of their town or city in large white letters on rooftops to aid pilots in navigation. She is the first woman to hold a government aviation post, serving as technical advisor to the National Advisory Committee for Aeronautics under President Franklin D. Roosevelt.

1921—Gertrude "Trudy" Ederle, fourteen, wins an international three-mile swim in New York Bay against fifty of the best swimmers of England and the United States.

1923—Of all U.S. colleges, 22 percent have varsity sports for women.

1924—Alexandra David-Neel of England is the first European woman to travel to Lhasa, the forbidden city in Tibet.

1924—Sybil Bauer becomes the first women to break an existing men's world swimming record when she wins the 100-metre backstroke at the Olympic Games.

1926—Kinue Hitomi, Japan's foremost woman athlete, wins two gold medals at the second World Women's Games.

1927—American Helen Wills wins her first of eight singles tennis titles at the All-England Club. She holds the number one world ranking for eight years. In her career, she captures a total of thirty-one career Grand Slam titles, including nineteen in singles.

1928—Nellie Zabel Whillhite solos, becoming South Dakota's first licensed woman pilot. She is probably the first pilot to be almost completely deaf. An outstanding air show performer, she excels at the tight, fast maneuvering necessary for balloon target racing, where pilots fly into balloons to burst them.